Alchemy and Meggy Swann

KAREN CUSHMAN

sandpiper

Houghton Mifflin Harcourt

Boston ◇ New York

SANDPIPER and the SANDPIPER logo are trademarks of Houghton
Mifflin Harcourt Publishing Company.

For information about permission to reproduce selections from this book,
write to Permissions, Houghton Mifflin Harcourt Publishing Company,
215 Park Avenue South, New York, New York 10003.

www.hmhbooks.com

The text of this book is set in Fairfield 45 Light.
Map by Kayley LeFaiver

The Library of Congress has cataloged the hardcover edition as follows:
Cushman, Karen.
Alchemy and Meggy Swann / by Karen Cushman.
p. cm.
Summary: In 1573, the crippled, scorned, and destitute Meggy Swann goes
to London, where she meets her father, an impoverished alchemist, and
eventually discovers that although her legs are bent and weak, she has
many other strengths.
[1. People with disabilities—Fiction. 2. Alchemy—Fiction. 3. Poverty—
Fiction. 4. Fathers and daughters—Fiction. 5. London (England)—
History—16th Century—Fiction. 6. Great Britain—History—Elizabeth,
1558–1603—Fiction.] I. Title.
PZ7.C962Al 2010
[Fic]—dc22
2009016387

ISBN: 978-0-547-23184-6 hardcover
ISBN: 978-0-547-57712-8 paperback

Manufactured in the United States of America
DOC 10 9 8 7 6 5 4 3 2 1

4500314328

❦ For Leah, ❦
for her gentle courage
and her tender heart

The meeting of two personalities is like
the contact of two chemical substances;
if there is any reaction, both are transformed.

—Carl Jung

❧ 1573 ❧

*After the accession of Elizabeth I
to the throne of England
but afore London's first theater
and Shakespeare*

Ye toads and vipers," the girl said, as her granny often had, "ye toads and vipers," and she snuffled a great snuffle that echoed in the empty room. She was alone in the strange, dark, cold, skinny house. The carter who had trundled her to London between baskets of cabbages and sacks of flour had gone home to his porridge and his beer. The flop-haired boy in the brown doublet who had shown her a straw-stuffed pallet to sleep on had left for his own lodgings. And the tall, peevish-looking man who had called her to London but did not want her had wrapped his disappointment around him like a cloak and disappeared up the dark stairway, fie upon him!

Fie upon them all!

She was alone, with no one to sustain and support her. Not even Louise, her true and only friend, who had fallen asleep in the back of the cart and been overlooked. Belike Louise was on her way back out of the town with the carter, leaving the girl here frightened and hungry and alone. Ye toads and vipers, what was she to do? She sat shivering on a stool as unsteady as her humor, and tears left shining tracks like spider threads on her cheeks.

Her name was Margret Swann, but her gran had called her Meggy, and she was newly arrived from Millford village, a day's ride away. The bit of London she had seen was all soot and slime, noise and stink, and its streets were narrow and dark. Now she was imprisoned in this strange little house on Crooked Lane. Crooked Lane. How the carter had laughed when he learned their destination.

Darkness comes late in high summer, but come it does. Meggy could see little of the room she sat in. Was there food here? A cooking pot? Wood for a fire? Would the peevish-looking man—Master Peevish, she decided to call him—would he come down and give her a better welcome?

Startled by a sudden banging at the door and in truth a bit fearful, Meggy stood up quickly, grabbed her walking sticks, and made her way into the farthest corner of the room. She moved in a sort of clumsy jig: reach one stick ahead, swing leg wide and drag it forward, move other stick ahead, swing other leg wide and drag it forward, over and over again, stick, swing, drag, stick, swing, drag. Her legs did not sit right in her hips—she had been born so—and as a result she walked with this awkward swinging gait. Wabbling, Meggy called it, and it did get her from one place to another, albeit slowly and with not a little bit of pain.

The banging came again, and then the door swung open and slammed against the wall, revealing the carter who had fetched her to London.

He was not gone! Meggy's spirits rose like yeasty bread, and she wabbled toward the doorway. "Well met, carter," she said. "I wish to go home."

"I were paid sixpence to bring you hither," he said. "Have you another six for the ride back?"

"Nay, but my mother—"

He shook his head. "Your mother was right pleased to see the back of you." He turned, took two steps, and lifted something from the bed of the wagon. Something that wriggled and hissed. Something that leapt from his arms. Something that showed itself to be a large white goose, her wings spread out like an angel's as she made her waddling way over to the girl. Louise. Meggy's goose and friend.

Meggy exhaled in relief and gladness. She bent down and looked into the goose's deep black eyes. "Pray be not angry with me, Louise. In all the hurly-burly of arriving, I grew forgetful." Louise honked loudly and shook herself with such a shake that there was a snowfall of feathers.

When Meggy stood up again, the carter and the wagon had gone. Her eyes filled, but her hands held tightly to her walking sticks, so she could not dash the tears away. They felt sticky on her lips, and salty.

She sat down on the stool again and put one arm around the goose, who stretched her neck and placed her head on

Meggy's lap. "You may observe, goosie," the girl said, stroking the soft, white head, "that I be most lumpish, dampnified, and right bestraught. This London is a horrid place, and I know not what will befall us here."

Meggy and Louise rocked for a moment, and Meggy softly sang a misery song she had learned from her gran. *I wail in woe, I plunge in pain, with sorrowing eyes I do complain,* she sang, but the sound of her trembly voice in the empty room was so mournful that she stopped and sat silent while darkness grew.

Meggy and the carter had arrived in London earlier that day while the summer evening was yet light. Even so, the streets were gloomy, with tall houses looming on either side, rank with the smell of fish and the sewage in the gutter, slippery with horse droppings, clamorous with church bells and the clatter of cart wheels rumbling on cobbles. London was a gallimaufry of people and carts, horses and coaches, dogs and pigs, and such noise that made Meggy's head, accustomed to the gentle stillness of a country village, ache.

"Good even', mistress," the carter had called to a hairy-chinned woman with a tray of fish hanging from her neck. "Know you where we might find the house at the Sign of the Sun?"

"I cannot seem to recall," the fishwife said, "but belike I'd remember if my palm were crossed with a penny." She stuck out a hand, knobby and begrimed. The carter frowned and grunted but finally took a penny from the purse tied at his waist and flicked it at her.

She plucked it from the air and flashed a gummy smile. "Up Fish Street Hill but a little ways is Crooked Lane," she said. "You will see the Sign of the Sun six or more houses up the lane."

Crooked Lane. Meggy had pulled her skirts tighter around her legs, and the carter had laughed.

As the fishwife had said, six houses up Crooked Lane, below a faded sign of, indeed, the sun, was the narrowest house Meggy had ever seen, hardly wider than a middling-tall man lying edge to edge, and three stories high. Its timbers were black with age, and the yellow plaster faded to a soft cream. A bay window on each floor was fitted with small panes of glass, dusty and spotted and, here and there, cracked. The upper floors hung over the street, as was true of all the houses in Crooked Lane, so the street was shadowy and damp. To one side of the house was a shop, shuttered and dark, with a large shoe hanging in front, betokening a cobbler's shop, Meggy thought. There was a bit of garden next to it, although what would grow in that damp gloom Meggy could not say. On the other side was a purveyor of old clothes. "Old cloaks? Have you an old cloak to sell?" the merchant called from the door of his shop. "Or mayhap—"

"Away, fellow," the carter said. "We have business with the master here."

The clothes seller snorted. "Business? With him? Abracadabra more like." And he spat.

Abracadabra? Meggy shivered now, remembering. "What could he have meant?" she asked Louise. But the goose, busily grooming her feathers, did not answer.

"And hearken to me, Louise," Meggy went on. "On London Bridge I beheld heads, people's heads, heads black with rot and mounted on sticks, hair blowing in the summer wind like flags at a fair. Traitors, the carter said, a lesson and a warning." The girl shivered again. Heads. What sort of place was this London?

As darkness grew, Meggy lay down carefully and with some difficulty and undertook to make herself comfortable on the straw pallet, she who had slept on Granny's goose-feather mattress. She did not know what hurt her most—her aching legs or her empty belly or her troubled heart. Pulling her cloak over her and nestling Louise beside her, she breathed in the familiar smell of goose and grew sleepy.

Mayhap this was but a bad dream, she thought. The dark, the cold, the strange noises, and the unfriendly man who had judged her, found her wanting, and left her alone—perhaps these were but part of a dream, and she would wake again in the kitchen of the alehouse. "Sleep well, Louise," said Meggy to her goose, "for tomorrow, I pray, we be home."

❧ T W O ❧

he heads on the bridge were the stuff of nightmares. Here was Louise's head, her black eyes cold and empty. And there Granny's gray hair blew in the wind. And this was Meggy's head, mouth open in a hopeless wail . . .

Meggy woke with a cry. The night had the quiet stillness of the hours after midnight but before dawn. Over the pounding of her heart, she could hear voices and footsteps upstairs. Was Master Peevish coming down? Was he sorry he had given her so poor a welcome?

He did not appear. Meggy tried to fall asleep again, but her mind returned to her encounter with the man when she had arrived. "I do not allow beggars at my house" was the first thing he said to her. "Begone and clear my doorstep."

"Pray pardon, sir, we are not beggars," the carter had told him. "If you be Master Ambrose, this be your daughter, come at your bidding."

The black-gowned man, tall and narrow like his house, peered down at the girl through eyes as dark as her own, nearly hidden by bushy black eyebrows as if two caterpillars slumbered on his brow. "Daughter?" he asked, frowning. The caterpillars woke and collided over his nose. "I expected a son."

A son. Not her. No more did she want him, this ill-favored, ill-mannered old man in a shabby black gown. Ye toads and vipers, what did she need with a father?

She turned to go, anxious to be otherwhere, but the carter held her arm. "I were told I would be paid sixpence for this delivery," he said, sticking out his hand. "Sixpence."

Master Ambrose pulled pennies from inside his gown and gave them to the carter, who turned for his wagon. Still frowning, Master Ambrose studied Meggy. "What are you called?"

A sudden breeze tugged at the hair that tumbled like storm clouds from her linen cap and tangled in her eyes and mouth. She said naught but only frowned back at the man's long face, the long nose, and those great bushy eyebrows. Her gran had admonished her often, "Do not greet the world with your fists up, sweeting. Give folk a chance." But her gran was dead, and Meggy was here, and her hands on her sticks clenched into fists.

The man and the girl stood in silence until he called to the carter, "God's wounds, is she mute? Or brain cracked?"

The carter shrugged once more as he climbed onto the wagon and tossed Meggy's sack over the side.

"Hold, fellow!" Master Ambrose shouted. "Hold. What use is a daughter to me?" But the carter merely clucked to his horse, which pulled the wagon up the street and away.

They stood for a long moment, the man in the doorway and Meggy on the step. Finally he turned and entered the house, leaving her to follow.

Brain cracked, he had called her. A daughter, not a son. Ye toads and vipers, he would have more disappointments to deal with this day, Meggy thought. She leaned on her walking sticks and, dipping and lurching, moved herself into the house—stick, swing, drag, stick, swing, drag—pain accompanying her every step.

The man turned and watched her, one caterpillar arching on his brow. Shoving past her, he strode back to the door and shouted after the wagon, "Good sir, hold, I said! The girl be . . . she cannot . . . I want . . ." But the wagon was disappearing up the darkening lane.

Master Ambrose sighed and closed the door. "I know not what I am to do with you. A son would be of use to me, but a daughter, and such a daughter . . ." He did not look at her but walked to the staircase in a corner of the room. "Roger," he called. "Roger, come down."

A young fellow a year or two older than Meggy, wearing brown doublet and hose of strawberry red, pounded down the stairs. He grinned at Meggy and his hair flopped into his eyes. "Roger," said Master Ambrose, "this be . . . err, my . . . err, daughter. See to her. I must return to my work."

The boy called Roger nodded as the man started up the stairs. Then the boy picked up Meggy's sack from the doorstep and said, "Go to! So the master has a daughter. I bid you welcome." But his grin faded as he gestured toward her walking sticks. "What means those?"

Meggy had had a long day. She had left her home and been bounced in a wagon over bumpy roads, assailed by smells and mud and noise, and then insulted by a man said to be her father. She was not in the best of humors. And now this boy was vexing her with his big eyes and his annoyous prattle. She pulled her face into a scowl and shook one of her walking sticks at him. "Beware the ugglesome crookleg, the foul-featured cripple, the fearful, misshapen creature," she growled, "marked by the Devil himself."

The boy backed up against the wall, but he did not run. In the village where Meggy was born, the children ran. Meggy seldom went among the villagers, but when she did, they jeered or shunned her, cursed and spat, and mothers pulled their toddlers behind their skirts for fear she would bewitch them with the evil eye. This boy did not run or spit or curse.

She narrowed her eyes. "Be you not afeared?" she asked him.

He stared at her solemnly but said nothing. He would come to fear her or taunt her or avoid her, Meggy knew. Everyone did. Everyone but Louise.

"My mother held that my crooked legs are the judgment of God upon me for my sins," Meggy said. "She bade me stay out of sight lest I curse our patrons and make the ale sour. *Now* be you afeared?"

He cocked his head, and his brown hair fell forward like the long ears of a spaniel pup. "Indeed I know not what to think of you," he said. "But you be my master's daughter, so take some comfort and rest." He moved a stool closer to where Meggy stood. "I cannot offer you a fire. The master will not spare the wood. But for the room at the top of the stairs, the rest of this house is cold as January all the year round."

He pointed to a straw pallet folded into a corner. "You can sleep on that. I found it lumpy and dusty, but it serves. The water bearer will come each sevennight, for it is clear you cannot fetch water yourself. And there is this." He gestured to the chamber pot beside the pallet and turned for the door.

"Nay, hold!" Meggy called. "You cannot abandon me. What am I to do here? Who will tend to me? And fetch me things to eat?"

"Belike you will fetch it yourself," Roger said. "Up Crooked Lane to Eastcheap you will find taverns, fruit-mongers, and bakers. Where Fish Street Hill changes to Gracechurch there be grocers and butchers. But closest are the cookshops and brewers on Thames Street, down Crooked Lane instead of up and toward the river to where Fish Street Hill meets the church of St. Magnus and—"

"Can you not see, rude sir, that I could ne'er walk all that way?" She waved her walking sticks at him. Because her legs often tormented her, she had to measure the gain of each journey against the pain—would the reward be worth it? Roger, the lack-witted woodsnape, could not understand that.

"Did you not walk and work and such in that village you came from?" he asked.

"I stayed out of the way, is what I did there. And there was ever bread in the alehouse kitchen when I grew hungry." She sighed loudly. "You will have to fetch me food."

The boy laughed. "I will see you anon," he said, "but now I must be off to supper and bed in my new lodgings." Sweeping his hat onto his head, he bade her a good even. He was laughing again as he left.

Now Meggy was alone, hungry and thirsty and frightened in the dark house in the middle of the night. Despair settled over her like the wings of a great dark bird. She pulled her cloak over her head and settled back into her nightmares.

Morning came at last, as it ever does. Ere Meggy opened her eyes, she listened for the familiar sounds of home—cock crow, breezes singing in the tall grass, cows lowing to be milked, the greetings and fare-thee-wells of travelers—but there were none such. Instead she heard church bells clanging, men arguing, the calls of peddlers and the screeching of gulls.

It had not been a dream. She was still in London, in the house of Master Peevish. She frowned. If he was her father, did that then make her Mistress Peevish? It suits me, I fear, she thought, and moved her lips in what might have been a tiny smile.

Leaning heavily on her sticks, she pulled herself up off the floor. She found the chamber pot and, cursing this little house that had no privy such as the alehouse had, she managed, with a great deal of arranging and rearranging, to use it. Opening the door, she threw the contents into the stinking ditch that flowed past the house and placed the pot back in the corner. She found a bit of wood in the street and used that to clean up after Louise, who had done in the night what geese do, and that, too, Meggy threw into the street. Then she folded the straw mat and put it next to the chamber pot.

Hunger and curiosity both poked at her, and she looked about. This seemed a poor, puny, paltry sort of house. There was but the one small room—no dining chamber, no kitchen, no pantry, no buttery for storage, no cupboard. Dust motes danced in the pale sunlight peeping through the window and settled on a lone wooden table and benches. The empty fireplace held no fire, no andirons, no pothooks or bellows or spit for meat. And nowhere was there aught to eat.

She had missed her supper the night before, although the boy Roger, fie upon him, had gone home to his. What was she to do to quiet her grumbling belly?

She longed for the alehouse where she had lived with her mother and her gran, poor and plain as it had been. She missed the scents of fresh ale and clean rushes and meat turning on the spit. This house stank of dust and mildew and, from somewhere, a foul reek like hen's eggs gone rotten. All in all it did not seem a place where people truly lived.

Meggy sat down at the table and drew an M in the dust on the top. Would Master Peevish come downstairs? Did he even recall that she was there? Would the boy in the brown doublet come back? She had not used him very kindly. He had seemed a friendly sort, but she cared not about being friends. People do not favor me, she thought, nor I them. "I need no friend but you, Louise. You do not mind that sometimes

I be Mistress Peevish," she said to the goose. "But what am I to do in this place? I have no food, no one to comfort or help or listen to me. Master Peevish would have an able-bodied son, not a crippled daughter. What am I to do?" Louise, of course, did not answer.

If she could find sixpence for the carter, she could return to the village and the alehouse, perhaps, but she would receive a cold welcome there. As the carter had remarked, her mother—the village alewife, known for her good ale and her bad temper—had not been sorry to see the girl go. "My mother cannot stomach me," Meggy had often said to Louise. "I might as well have two heads, like the calf born on Roland Pigeon's farm."

Once it was apparent that Meggy would be lame, she had been put in the care of her gran, who dwelt in rooms over the alehouse stable. Sweet Granny, with gnarled hands and a face like a pickle, had given her love and warmth and kept her mostly out of sight. It was her gran who had found likely sticks in the woods and showed the girl how to use them for walking. But Granny had died two winters past, and without her broad back and strong arms to carry the girl up and down the ladder in the stable, Meggy had to return to the alehouse and her mother.

And then yestermorn, just afore dawn, "Your father, master at the Sign of the Sun in London, has bid you come to him," her mother had said. "You leave this morning."

"Nay, 'tis not so," said Meggy. "I have no father." Certes she had a father; everyone has a father. But never in her thirteen years had Meggy heard her mother speak of him. Her gran had merely said, "You have a mother who feeds you and a gran who loves you. What need have you of a father?" Still, Meggy had at times wondered and imagined what and where this father was. Was he tall? Lean limbed or swag bellied? Did he smell of wood smoke and horses or of ink and musty books? Did he have black hair like hers? Was he, too, lame?

"Why have you ne'er told me of him?" Meggy had asked her mother yestermorn. "Why has he been so long gone, and why am I to go to him now?"

Her mother shrugged. "Belike you will find out soon enough."

And so Meggy was in London, unwanted by father as well as mother. What was she to do? Ye toads and vipers.

~⚞ T H R E E ⚟~

Meggy lingered there, thinking and fretting, until, with a slam of the big wooden door, Roger bounced into the room.

So he had come back. Meggy thought he looked ever more like a puppy, all friendliness and no brains. She was relieved and annoyed and mightily hungry, but all she said was "Ahh, methought I heard the door open and a mighty wind blow in. What will you, puppy?"

"See what I have brought, fresh from the larder of Mistress Grimm." He unfolded a cloth from around a heel of bread and a hunk of yellow cheese and handed her a bit of each. "I had to draw a sword and fight a rat for the cheese, but I vanquished him, and here it be." Not knowing whether he jested or not, Meggy inspected her bit of cheese for marks of rat teeth.

The boy fetched a mug from the windowsill. "You must drink from clay, I fear. The master has melted or sold all the metal in the house." That explained the lack of andirons, pots, and pothooks, Meggy thought, but why would he do so?

The boy poured some of the ale from the tankard he carried into Meggy's mug. "Have you seen him this day?" he asked, sitting across from her at the table.

She shook her head but said naught, her mouth full of bread.

"In sooth 'tis a poor welcome he has given you," the boy said, "but you will grow accustomed to his ways in time. He can be forgetful, his head filled with philosophy and such, and sometimes he be frosty as a winter night, though he will not beat you or berate you overmuch." He stood up suddenly and smacked his head with his hand. "But I forget my manners. Roger Oldham, if it please you, mistress," he said with a small bow.

"Old-dumb?"

"No, Old-ham. O-L-D as in old, H-A-M as in, well, ham."

"Or pork. Or pigmeat. Well, Roger Old-pigmeat, I am Margret Swann," said Meggy after swallowing. "And this is Louise," she added, gesturing toward the goose, who waddled up to Roger and nipped him on his knee.

"Hellborn bird!" Roger shouted. "She has bitten me!" He sat down again and rubbed his leg as Louise, with a great fluff of her feathers, settled herself.

"I think she simply be curious about how you taste," said Meggy.

"If she does not leave off my leg, I will be knowing how *she* tastes," he responded.

"I pray you, Master Oldmeat, no roast goose jests where Louise might hear." The girl took another great bite of bread and asked through a mouthful, "Are you servant here?"

Still rubbing his leg, Roger shook his head. "Nay, no longer. I was two years setting fires and sweeping ashes, fetching food from the cookshop and water from the conduit, washing linen and airing clothes, shopping for beakers and bottles, powders and potions, and assisting the master in his work. Now I go elsewhere, so he summons you."

"He wants me to be his servant? That is why he called for me?" Meggy trembled with anger and disappointment. "I cannot be a servant. My legs are crooked and my arms busy with my sticks. Walking pains me, and climbing, and standing. I go seldom among strangers, for they spit and curse at me, and this London makes my head ache." She struggled to her feet. "A pox on it. Go and tell your master that I have left his house and will trouble him no more. And he can make a hundred able-bodied sons to serve him—it matters not to me."

"Whither go you?"

"I know not."

"How get you there?"

"I care not." Meggy threw her arms into the air in a careless motion, and her sticks clattered to the floor. She sat down again. 'Twas bravely spoken, but in truth she was all unknowing and fearful about what would befall her outside this house at the Sign of the Sun.

Roger handed her the sticks. Meggy frowned at him. "Why are you not afeared of me?" she asked. "Have you not the wit?"

The boy scowled but spoke mildly. "My father was physician in Cambridge, where men look not to God and demons for explanations but rather to natural principles and bodily causes." He was silent a moment and then added, "In truth, I think you as friendly as a bag of weasels but too small to be dangerous."

Meggy banged a stick against the floor again. "Be not daft, servant boy," she said. "I be most dangerous, a fearsome cripple who delights in affrighting people."

"I have no toddling babe to be marked or cattle to be cursed. I be not overfond of you but I am not afeared." Roger lifted his tankard from the table and raised it to Meggy. "Does that discomfit you?"

It did. It also alarmed and pleased and confounded her. She sought a new topic. "You said you shopped for powders and potions. Be the master a physician?"

"Nay, he deals not with humours and remedies but with matter, with metals, with liquids and vapors."

"Is he a perfumer?"

"Not at all. He is a learned man."

"An apothecary?"

Roger shook his head. "The master does seek to discover the secrets of the universe, of all matter, and how its essence can be changed."

"Go to! He is a magician," Meggy said, and shivered at the thought. Abracadabra.

"Nay, he is an alchemist," Roger said, "a master of the art of transformation."

Meggy was relieved to hear there was no magic in the

house. "I have heard of such men, who claim to change straw into gold," she told Roger. "Is he then rich? This does not look like a rich man's house."

"'Tis metal, lead and such, that alchemists try to transform into gold, and no, he is not rich. He uses all he earns for his work." Roger put some pennies on the table. "Here is all that is left of the coins he gave me last for food. 'Tis meager indeed, and you will have much ado to get more from him. Easier to get soup from a stone than money from a philosopher."

"Philosopher? You just now said he is an alchemist."

The boy took a large bite of bread and washed it down with another mouthful of ale before speaking. "Alchemy is a hodgepodge enterprise, a good deal philosophy, with a bit of smelting, a little distilling, even boiling and brewing. Also calcination and percolation."

"Enough, puppy. Just what does he *do* in the rooms upstairs?"

"He searches for the *aqua vitae*, the elixir of life that can rid substances of their impurities and make all things perfect." Roger took another bite of bread. "Transformation, he says it is, changing things in their essence."

"And that will turn metal into gold?"

Roger nodded.

"You have seen him do it?" Meggy asked.

"Nay, he still has not the method, although he swears he is close to finding it."

Picturing the man's long, peevish face and shabby gown, Meggy shook her head. "Belike 'tis but a pretty dream. I shall not believe until I see him with a handful of gold. And tell me, when *shall* I see him?"

Roger shrugged. "The master labors at his Great Work from dawn until dark and from dark until dawn. He rests little and eats seldom. When he wants you, he will call."

Meggy dipped a bit of bread in the mug of ale and threw it to Louise. The ale was cool and wet, but not nearly tasty enough to please the daughter of an alewife. "In sooth I cannot be his servant," she said to Roger, "so you must stay and serve us both."

"Nay, not a moment longer than necessary," he said. "I go to a new life, and most glad I am of it."

"That man upstairs does not want me. I will go with you."

"You cannot. I go to be a player in the company of the esteemed Cuthbert Grimm and Dick Merryman."

Meggy knew about players. They often stayed in the rooms above the alehouse. Her mother cursed their rowdiness and examined their coins carefully lest they try to cheat her. Why would Roger wish to be such a rogue? "I believe players are disreputable and dishonest and should be whipped from the town."

"Nay, Mistress Margret, players are men most like gods. They comfort the sad, amuse the wealthy, inspire the common," he said, gesturing wildly. "We players put poetry onstage, telling stories about men great and ordinary, about their deeds and their misfortunes, revealing their very hearts and souls."

"And you are paid wages for this?"

"Certes we are," he said, looking pleased with himself.

"Belike I could learn to be a player," Meggy said. "My legs are weak but my wits are not."

Roger shook his head. "Nay, mistress."

Her blood grew hot. "Because I am lame?"

"Nay, because you are female. Females cannot be players."

"Why say you that?"

"Because 'tis so."

"Go to! What stories have no females?"

"We younger players take the women's parts. I myself will be Lady Emma when we play *The Tragic Tale of King Ethelred the Unready*."

Meggy snorted. "You, Roger Oldham, old ham, old meat, ancient pork, you play a woman? With your big feet and your knightly nose?"

Roger smiled. "I do make a somewhat lordly woman." Meggy started to speak, but Roger shook his head again and said, "Nay, Mistress Margret, nay, you cannot come with me."

Meggy felt her lip threaten to tremble. "But what will befall me here alone? Belike I will sink under my afflictions."

Roger stood. "I board in the house of Cuthbert Grimm next to Peter Ragwort the butcher on Pudding Lane. It does stink a fair bit but keeps the rain off. If you have need of me, seek me there."

He was leaving her! He had eaten supper but brought her only old bread and moldy cheese! Pigeon pie he ate, no doubt, and custard. She stiffened with anger. "Fie upon you, Roger Oldmeat! I will seek you when pigs grow wings! A pox on your players and your poetry and your Cuthbert Grimm!"

She threw the last bit of her bread at his head, although she would regret its loss later. "Haste then away. Would that I ne'er see your silly grin again."

And, by cock and pie, not saying another word, he left her alone in the house at the Sign of the Sun.

Without Roger the room felt darker and cold. Meggy sought a candle or even a rushlight, hoping to dispel the gloom in the room and in her heart, but found none. The house at the Sign of the Sun indeed. More like the house at the sign of the gloom, she thought. "Why think you this dark house has the Sign of the Sun?" she asked Louise.

Louise ignored her and began to groom her feathers, fluffy as thistledown and lily white.

"Belike," Meggy continued, "someone wanted to bring a bit of light and heat into this dark dreariness."

She went to the window and tried to see through the grime. Leaning close, she spat and rubbed the glass with the hem of her kirtle. There was gray gloom outside as well as in. Ye toads and vipers, it be summer, Meggy thought. Where were the billows of grain, thickets of berries and wild plums, the roses, poppies, and fields of daisies? This London was a poor place, and she longed to go home.

Although it was but midday, she spread the pallet Roger had given her before the fireplace again and lay down. She'd get no warmth from an empty fireplace, she knew, but still it comforted her to be there.

❦ FOUR ❧

When Meggy woke, it was not yet evening. Roger's cheese was long gone and she was hungry again. She knew of no food in the house but for the dry and dirty lump of bread she had heaved at the boy. Ye toads and vipers, you could play my belly like a drum, she thought, 'tis that empty.

She had not seen Master Peevish again, although she had heard whispering and footsteps coming and going in the night. Or had she been dreaming?

A rumble from her belly finally sent Meggy reaching for her walking sticks. Might she do it? Could she wabble to a cookshop by the river to spend the pennies Roger had left her? Fie upon it, had he said down Crooked Lane or up? Exactly where was Gracechurch Street? And was she to go past the church of St. Magnus or turn a corner there?

"Stay you here, Louise," she said. "If that man comes down, keep out of sight. I will return with supper. Mayhap I will find something we can share—fresh berries or pear tart or sweet apple cake with nuts." Her mouth watered at the thought.

Meggy emptied her sack of her few belongings—comb, small knife for eating, clean smock, a kirtle of Bristol red, a pair of stockings with the toes mended into a bunch, and a bottle of onion, fig, and Venice treacle tonic against plague. Her gran had sewn handles on a grain sack so that Meggy could loop it over her arm, leaving her hands free for her sticks. She put the sack to her face and sniffed deeply. Her eyes filled with tears. It smelled of home.

Sighing, Meggy took the sack, tucked the coins into her bodice, and peeked out the door. The warmth of the day surprised her after the chill of the house, and streaks of sunshine found their way even to Crooked Lane. She would sooner have waited for dark, when she would be seen less easily, but she was hungry now.

She looked up the lane and down. The old-cloaks man was arranging the boots and hose and doublets in the stall attached to his shop. Certes he would know where she could buy a sausage pie or baked apple. But he was a stranger. Dare she speak to him? She cleared her throat and called, "I give you good day, sir."

He turned, looked at Meggy, and spat. "Hellfire and damnation, I say, to cursed cripples, evil and ugglesome, who defile the streets with their dark arts! Hellfire!" He spat again.

She turned away from him and her eyes grew hot. Would that I were a tool of the Devil, she thought, for belike he could keep people from shouting and cursing at me in the streets.

She wabbled slowly down the lane, passing the shop marked with a shoe. There was no sign of the cobbler. Meggy hoped he would permit Louise to feed on the grass and greens that grew in his garden. Worse than thunder, Meggy thought, worse than biting flies, worse than demons that howl in the night, is a hungry goose.

Crooked Lane was well named. Horrid steep it was, and it curved and curved again. By the time she reached the bottom, Meggy's legs burned and her knees trembled. Oh woeful day, she thought, overflowing with pity for herself, I will ne'er find a food shop but belike will expire here on the street and be mourned by no one. Yet the scent of sizzling sausages from somewhere summoned her on.

At its end, the lane met a large thoroughfare that Meggy recalled from yesterday. Fish Street Hill it was, cobbled instead of muddy but still wet and slick. She zigged and zagged to avoid the slops puddling in the street and at times raining down from the upper stories of houses on both sides.

Every corner swarmed with people: peddlers and rat catchers, toy merchants and dung collectors, silken-cloaked ladies and children in ragged breeches, all going about their lives, laughing, shouting, arguing, jeering, and jostling. Carts and carriages thundered by, their wheels splashing her skirts.

Apprentices pulled her about, urging her to buy this and try that. "Good mistress, follow me," said one young fellow, tugging at her. "My master's shop offers the finest cloth, the silkiest ribbons, the sharpest pins."

"Want any ink? Do you want any ink?" asked another.

"Have you any old boots to sell?" clamored a third.

"What do ye lack? What do ye lack?" vendor after vendor called after her until her head was spinning. And when she did not stop, each added, as she always expected, "crookleg" or "monstrous child" or "ill-formed wench."

"Come and buy," a ballad seller called, "a new ballad of Robin Hood." And the man began to sing: *Others may tell you of bold Robin Hood, derry derry down, or else of the barons bold, but I will tell you how he served the bishop when he robbed him of his gold.*

Meggy joined in: *Derry derry, hey! Derry derry down!* for she knew the ballad well.

The ballad seller winked at her as he walked on, singing: *Derry derry derry derry down.*

Meggy walked on also, toward the cookshops on Thames Street, or was it St. Magnus Street, and did Roger not say something about Gracechurch? Meggy thought she had come a very great distance, stumbling now and again when her sack thumped against her knees or tangled with her walking sticks, but still she did not see the river ahead of her. Or behind her. So different was London from her village, where there was but one road in and one road out and no one lost his way.

She turned down a street, narrower and darker, and wabbled past a crowd of children. "Behold Mistress Duck," one of them cried. "Waddle, waddle, Mistress Duck!" Mimicking Meggy's walk, they followed behind her.

"By my faith, freaks!" someone called from a window. "From Bartlemas Fair belike. You there, crookleg. Know you the pig woman and the fish-scaled boy?"

Turning to her followers, Meggy gave them the awful face that frightened children in her village, and cried, "Curses on you, curses!" She raised a stick to shake at them but slipped and nearly fell into the street. The children only laughed as they stumbled away, shaking their fists and shouting to each other, "Curses! Curses on you!"

Meggy ducked into an alley that proved quieter and less crowded. She leaned against a building to rest her legs. The thought of facing more stares, frowns, and harsh words held her back. Should she return to the house at the Sign of the Sun unfed? Her empty belly rumbled, "No." She tried to recall what Roger had said about Thames Street and the river, but she was well and truly lost.

The narrow passage she had entered was dark and slippery with slime. More gutter than street, it reeked of old fish and new dung. There must be another way. She was turning to go when a voice from a doorway called, "Here, girl, I have perch, or mayhap it is flounder. It be yours for a penny." A man in ragged jerkin and hose held out a fish, its eyes popping, its scales dull, its odor insufferable. "Here. 'Tis fresh."

"Nay, 'tis not, but as far from fresh as I am far from home," Meggy said, "and I will not—"

"Are you saying I lie, crooked legs?" he asked, stepping

closer. Meggy backed away, up against a wall. "Give me a penny and take this fish."

"Nay. Begone, you—"

"Then I will take me this instead," he said, grabbing at her sack. "And these." Her walking sticks!

"Vile thief! Beastly villain!" Meggy shouted. "Let loose my sticks!" But as she reached for them, she slipped and fell aspraddle on the street. Would she die in this dark, reeking alley, unable to get back to the house where Master Peevish did not want her anywise? Would this be her end, a helpless cripple huddled against a wall?

Tears of anger and self-pity slithered down her cheeks. In her dreams she danced and ran, but only in her dreams. In this fetid alley she could not even fight back. It was Roger's fault for making her fetch her own food, she thought. Would he even think to look for her?

A strange voice roared, "Begone, you carbuncled toad!" The newcomer grabbed Meggy's walking sticks from the thief and used one to club him on the head. "A pestilence take you, you rump-faced knave, out for thievery." The thief dropped Meggy's sack and skulked away.

"You," the man said, helping Meggy to her feet, "are a piteous spectacle." He handed her the walking sticks. "Be you hurt?"

"Aye, I be hurt indeed," she shouted, more angry than grateful. "I be crippled! Crooked! I could not defend me nor even walk away." She swung round to face her rescuer. He was dark, tall but bent, bony as a herring, with a scar on his face that puckered his cheek, squinting one eye and pulling his mouth into a lopsided sneer.

Ye toads and vipers, Meggy thought, I am delivered from a thief by a monster! She backed away.

The man frowned. "You should not be here," he said. "Mark me, you ask for trouble." He bent down and retrieved her sack. "Go home. Make haste," he said, handing it to her.

Meggy wiped tears from her face. "In truth I would if I knew whither it was."

"I am for Fish Street Hill. Might you find your way from there?"

She nodded.

"Then follow me." He strode off, and Meggy struggled to keep him in sight as she followed. Alleys became streets, and streets became wider and noisy with crowds: country folk in russet and broadcloth, sailors and soldiers in boothose and leather jerkins, young women with French hoods and feathered fans. Hawkers cried every sort of food: apples and pears, carrots and cowcumbers, fat salmon, pigs' trotters, chunks of cheese, and ginger cakes. A pig's head mounted on a stake, eyes bulging and mouth grinning, proclaimed a food stall, fragrant with spices, onions, and roasting meat. Ye toads and vipers! Here were the food vendors Roger had promised. But she feared to ask the ugly man to stop, so she limped on, anxious to be safe in Crooked Lane.

At Fish Street Hill they parted, and Meggy began the climb up Crooked Lane. She was nearly home, dizzy with relief and hunger, and there was Old Cloaks again, closing up his shop. "A pox on you, moldwort," she shouted at the man afore he had a chance to curse or to spit, "and a plague, and an ague, and . . . and . . . and the pukes!" Her belly might still be empty, but the rest of her felt better for the shouting.

Hearing laughter behind her, Meggy turned. She squinched her eyes and clenched her hands into fists. "Do you think to curse at me as well?" she asked of a yellow-haired man who stood at the door of the shop with the sign of the shoe.

"Not at all, mistress. That was well said. The fellow can be moldwort indeed."

The man was small and freckled, and his hair, Meggy saw, was not yellow but the red of a sunset roofed with a layer of sawdust. "Are you the cobbler?" she asked him.

He shook his head, and sawdust flew about him like moths around a torchlight. "The cobbler has been gone since the time of King Richard," he said. "'Tis but his sign that remains. I be, at your service, a cooper. Want you a barrel or a cask, a hogshead, firkin, rundlet, or tun, a bucket or tub or butter churn, I be your man." He looked at Meggy's sticks but said naught. Neither did he spit. "But you are in need of a cobbler?"

"Nay, Master Cooper," said Meggy. "I am neighborer, new come to lodge with the master there." She pointed to the house at the Sign of the Sun. "Margret Swann, if it please you." Then, surprising herself, she added, "Called Meggy, if you will."

The cooper nodded. "Welcome to Crooked Lane, Meggy Swann. I have heard tales of wondrous doings within your house. The search for mysterious substances. Magic and marvels."

31

"Truly? I have seen naught but darkness and dirt." She wished Master Peevish would indeed discover the elixir he sought. Mayhap he could use it on his own self and transform himself into a better father.

The smell of spice cake baking wafted from inside the cooper's shop. Meggy took a deep sniff. "Do I keep you from your supper, sir?" she asked.

"Nay, that is but the fine aroma of oak casks after firing. Since my good wife died, my son and I eat poorly. We will sup as usual on bread and cold roasted onions." The very words made Meggy's belly rumble. She thought to ask for a bit of bread, but she was no beggar—not for herself, although she did ask if Louise might feast on the greens in his yard. The cooper nodded again and went back inside his shop.

Louise was sitting on the window ledge when Meggy entered, and the bird flapped her wings mightily to show her displeasure at being left behind. "Mark me well, Louise," Meggy said, "this is a horrid city. You are fortunate that you can dine in the yard and not have to search through dark and dangerous alleys for something to fill your belly." She took the goose outside. "Still, hungry as I am, I have no desire to dine on grass and grit."

✲ F I V E ✲

Meggy and Louise had not been back more than a minute when Master Ambrose stepped suddenly from the stairs into the room, holding a candle. His eyes shone in the light like ripe blackberries. "Where is Roger?" he asked.

"He is not here, sir," Meggy said, "but has gone to the house of Master Grimm and . . . someone."

He waved his arm, and hot candle wax spattered Meggy's hand. "I gave him no leave to go."

"Shall I—"

"Fie upon him!" And the man turned and went back up the stairs, leaving Meggy alone in the dark.

"But . . . but . . . but . . ." Meggy said. She sat down and examined the wax on her hand. It hurt, she thought, so I must be here, even if he does not see me.

To quiet her hunger, she laid herself down on her pallet, although late-day light still peeked through the dirt on the windows. But her mistemper kept her from sleep. The man had sent for her and now ignored her. He was cold as a codfish, an unfeeling lout, a stale old mouse-nibbled piece of dried cheese. She had not expected much of this sudden father, but she had gotten even less. She would not stay with him. But where would she go? How could she survive? She had already made a bumble of her search for something to eat.

Her legs tormented her, her scratches and scrapes stung, and her stomach rumbled like a cart. The house was full of strange noises—creaking of timbers and rattling of windows, footsteps thudding on the floorboards above, the whispers of men who came and went in the dark. What would befall her here? Hot tears began again. I weep so much of late, she thought, 'tis as if I carry an onion in my sleeve.

At last she fell into a fretful sleep and dreamed of sausages that teased and tempted and then ran from her. Startled, Meggy woke to singing at the window, but it proved only the watchman on his rounds. "Twelve o'clock," he cried, "look well to your lock, your fire and your light, and so good night." She slept again, feeling not quite so alone. And thus ended Meggy's second day in the house at the Sign of the Sun.

She woke to soft rain. She stretched, and her belly rumbled with hunger. She had seen London. She had seen beggars and sailors and women with skirts like great seagoing ships, hobbyhorse peddlers and ballad sellers and pigs' heads on sticks, but she had seen little she wanted and no place where she belonged. She berated God and Roger, fortune and her father, for leaving her helpless and unwanted in this place.

When next she saw Master Peevish, she would address him. "Your pardon, sir, I have been awondering wherefore you sent for me" would be the most polite utterance, "I thought you wished me here, but you do not, and what am I to do now?" the most disappointed, and "Oh ye toads and vipers, you are as poor a parent as my mother. I wish my gran were alive" the most true.

Louise hissed a hiss that meant she wished to visit the garden plot next door for her breakfast. "Pray remember to eat some grit for your gizzard," Meggy told her as they went out, "lest your belly ache."

Louise honked in agreement.

As they tarried in the garden, a small boy came out of the cooper's shop and called, "Be that your goose?"

He was a stranger, but a very small stranger, with ears like a jug and the same red hair as the cooper. He did not seem to have a store of stones handy, nor was he poised to flee.

Meggy nodded. "Aye. I call her Louise. And who might you be?"

"I am Nicholas," he said. "I have no goose, but I do have me a horse. This is Charger." He presented a small horse carved of wood and gaily painted. "He is a mighty steed and runs fast as the wind."

Meggy went closer. "'Pon my honor," she said, "he looks very swift indeed."

The boy watched her walk up to him, stick, swing, drag. "Why do you walk with sticks?"

He did not ask in a taunting manner but quite simply, and Meggy surprised herself by answering in the same way. "Their strength makes up for my weak legs."

"Why does your goose ever have her wings spread out like that?"

"Louise is as lame as I am. She cannot fold her wings against her," Meggy said, "and she cannot fly. We are condemned to walk this earth with the same waddling gait. Belike that is why we be such friends."

"I would that I waddled also," said the boy, taking a few waddling steps.

"Nay, do not say that. I know I would rather walk, and certes Louise would fly if she could."

"Why?" Nicholas asked.

"Why do you ask so many questions?" she asked him in return.

"My father says I am curious as a jay," the boy said. And he smiled a gap-toothed, satisfied smile.

Out of one eye Meggy saw Master Peevish leave the house and hurry up the lane. Whither did he go? she wondered. And how long might he be gone? Perhaps Meggy could discover what mysterious things happened in the upper rooms without encountering him. If she could climb the stairs. And perhaps she might find a crust of bread there. Or a dusty almond cake. Or a withered apple. Even such leavings were beginning to sound appealing. If she could climb the stairs.

Meggy bade farewell to the cooper's boy and hurried Louise into the house. "Remain you here, Louise," she told the goose. "I will return anon."

The girl lumbered slowly up each step, stopping to rest

often. This will take a goodly long time, Meggy thought, so I pray his errand takes longer.

The next floor, as she had assumed, was the man's chamber. Naught but a bed with threadbare coverings, a clothes press with a broken lid, and six more steps. At the top of those stairs was a door, which, when pushed, swung open with a sound like a sigh. The attic room was smoky from a low-banked fire burning in a small earthen furnace, and dark, despite the tall window, for the glass was besmirched with spider webs and encrusted with dirt. The air was thick with the odors of ancient dust and candle wax, spoiled eggs, and sharp-smelling things for which Meggy had no name.

Leaning carefully on her sticks, Meggy moved into the room. Shelves were crammed to bursting with a hodgepodge that overflowed onto the floor: kettles and pitchers, stands and tongs, little jars full of queer-smelling things, and the skulls and bones of various small animals. There were clay bottles labeled in a language the girl could not read, although she had most of her letters; odd copper jugs with long spouts; and strange-looking vessels made of glass. Books, greasy with candle drippings, were piled on a rickety table and on the floor, higgledy-piggledy like the houses in Crooked Lane. For all she was small as a garden pea, Meggy feared she could not move without putting something in danger of ruination.

Just what did the man here? What was mixed in those bowls and cooked in that furnace? She could see nothing perfect and certainly no gold. Meggy longed to curl up near the warmth of the furnace, but the smellsome air burned her nose.

She found naught in the room to eat and so she turned to go, near colliding with a man looming in the doorway. "What do you in my laboratorium?" Master Ambrose asked in a voice that thundered in the small room. "I do not believe I gave you leave to enter, err, mistress."

Startled, Meggy stumbled into a shelf of glass implements. Before she could steady it, a beaker tipped and fell toward the floor. The alchemist reached out one long arm and caught it. "Clumsy girl, this glass be fragile and most costly."

Meggy's heart thumped. The man was so tall and his eyes so fierce that all sense left her. "I . . . I . . . I . . ." she stammered.

He put the glass beaker back on the shelf. "God save me," he murmured, "she is crippled, clumsy, and mute."

Meggy bristled. "Praying your pardon, sir," she said, "I am hardly mute. You but frighted me."

The man leaned closer. "Do you meddle in my things?"

She might have come uninvited, but she did not meddle. "Nay, sir, I was but curious. Never have I known someone engaged in a Great Work."

The man pulled at his earlobe, once, twice, three times, and then said, "So you be neither mute nor addlewitted. Mayhap I—"

Just then, with a great squawk, Louise climbed the last of the stairs and burst into the room, not around but over the books and flasks and bottles on the floor. She stepped into a basket, which fastened itself to her foot, and flapped noisily about, the basket slapping against the floor with each step.

"Louise!" Meggy called. "Come hither to me!" But the goose tripped and plunged her head into one of the precious glass vessels, and there was yet more flapping and flopping as Meggy frantically called, "Have done, Louise, have done! Put it down!"

Louise could not put it down but, bemaddened by her head being stuck in the beaker, stumbled about the room, knocking into another stack of books, the chair, and assorted devices of strange design, Master Ambrose lumbering after her. He finally penned the goose into a corner but could not pull her head out of the beaker. Shouting "A pox on you, you beetle-brained fowl!" he grabbed one of Meggy's walking sticks and swung it sharply at the goose's head, breaking the beaker and freeing her. Shards of glass sprayed like drops of dew. Louise honked again and flapped her great wings mightily.

"What creature is this?" Master Ambrose shouted. "What does it here?"

"That be Louise," Meggy said. "She is not accustomed to being a house goose."

Master Ambrose tore the cap from his head and threw it on the floor. "I wish not to see that bird," he shouted, "until it be roasted on a platter with onions and parsley!"

"Nay, sir, nay." Meggy shook her head fiercely. "Louise be not supper. She is my—"

"I care not. Hie it to a butcher," Master Ambrose said, "or I will dispatch it mine own self. Now leave my laboratorium."

Laboratorium? More likely stinkatorium, Meggy thought. She took her stick from the man and, shooing Louise before her, left the attic room. As she made her slow and painful way down the stairs, she told the goose, "You have made no little trouble for yourself, Louise. And for me." Louise, indifferent to the tumult she had provoked, merely flapped her wings and honked as she followed Meggy down.

❧ SIX ❧

Meggy peeped out the window onto Crooked Lane. She was sore afraid to venture back out into that London where she had been menaced by tradesmen, affrighted most grievously, and nearly dispatched by barbarous villains. But she could not ignore her father's threat to butcher Louise. What was she to do?

As the goose searched through her feathers for a bug or a flea or some other treat, the girl watched her and smiled. Louise had been her true friend since Meggy had saved her from the ax long ago, when it was discovered that her wings were slipped. Louise had followed Meggy about the inn yard, listened to her stories and songs, shared berries in the summer and apples in the fall. The girl and the goose were companions in their aloneness, their lameness, and their bad temper.

Meggy would save Louise if she could, but she feared disobeying Master Peevish. She would have to go back into the dust, mud, soot, slime, and smut of London. Roger had spoken of a butcher next to his lodgings on Pudding Lane. That was where they would go.

"Louise," Meggy said, "you are a flap-mouthed nuisance, but what shall I do without you?" Ripping a strip of cloth from her undersmock, Meggy tied it around Louise's neck for a leash. She put on her cloak, took up her walking sticks, slipped her sack over one arm, and pulled Louise from the house. The goose honked in irritation.

Could Meggy surrender Louise? She thought again of Master Peevish's anger. "Pray forgive me, Louise," Meggy told her. "It must be, but by my faith, I will miss you most fiercely."

The rain had lessened, but still the afternoon was wet, with mist rising off the river. Shop signs swung and banged in the wind as Meggy and Louise turned from Crooked Lane to Fish Street Hill. The girl and the goose stood in the fragrant steam rising from an inn. Meggy sniffed deeply for a moment. But might it be the aroma of roast goose she enjoyed? Her shoulders slumped.

"Pork pie, mistress," said a voice at her side. "Sweet with cinnamon and still hot from the baking." It was a girl, no bigger than Meggy, which meant she was very small indeed. And in the basket she carried were pies, brown of crust and fragrant. Meggy yet had the pennies Roger had given her, so she bought two pies. She ate one right there. The crust crumbled deliciously against her teeth, and meaty juices bespattered her chin.

The peddler nodded toward Meggy's sticks. "My old gran had such. For whipping me as much as for walking." The girl grinned a friendly grin.

While putting the other pie in her sack for later, Meggy asked, "Know you Pudding Lane where there be a butcher?"

The girl nodded. "Down the hill here to St. Magnus Church at Thames Street and then east to Pudding Lane. Likely you will smell it afore you see it." The two girls nodded to each other and walked on, the peddler in search of another penny and Meggy toward the butcher on Pudding Lane.

Louise hissed and spat and tried to pull away, but Meggy pulled harder. A pack of dogs wrangling over a bit of refuse left off their tussling to follow them, barking and nipping at Louise and at Meggy's walking sticks. They attracted several onlookers, cheering and calling, "Is there to be a show?" and "I wager tuppence on the goose!" It seemed that even more of an entertainment than a crippled girl was a crippled girl leading an angry goose.

Finally they turned onto Thames Street, where the crowds were more interested in their arguing, drinking, buying, and selling than in following a girl and her goose. Louise, tired of tuggling about London, sat herself down, her mighty wings trembling with outrage. "Come, Louise, cease your drumbling," Meggy said, pulling on the leash. But the goose only sat and squawked.

"Fie upon you, Louise Goose. 'Pon my honor, you are a true-bred nuisance," the girl said, leaning against a wall to rest.

A shepherd hurried past with his dogs and a herd of sheep, followed by a woman with a crowd of quarreling children. The woman could use a dog or two to manage that herd of hers, Meggy thought.

"Come buy a ballad newly made," a passing ballad seller called. "Mayhap 'The Ballad of Good Wives' or 'The Lover and the Bird.' Or come to me for the tale of a monstrous child born this very month to a weaver in Derbyshire. A child with one head but four arms and four legs. Printed at the Sign of the Jolly Lion this morn. Here to me. Come and buy." He waved the broadside about as he moved on. "Or buy a ballad newly writ. *God send me a wife that will do as I say*," he sang. "Come buy a ballad. Ha'penny, only a ha'penny." A sack holding a great number of the printed ballads hung down his back, and the man's arms passed through two handles, leaving his hands free to grab at passersby.

Meggy watched the ballad singer go and an idea blossomed. She took the second pork pie from the sack, shared it with Louise, and wiped her hands on her kirtle. Then, while Louise was distracted by the taste of pie, Meggy put the goose into the empty sack and tied the leash around the sack and the goose as if it were a package. Once she understood her predicament, the goose began to wiggle and hiss and try to free herself, but Meggy crouched down, placed the sack on her back over her shoulders, put her arms through the handles, just as the ballad seller had done, and carefully stood up, taking the weight on her shoulders. If she leaned heavily on her sticks and ignored the grumbling of her legs and Louise's frantic *hwonk-hwonk-hwonk,* she would be able to walk carrying the goose.

A blue-capped apprentice called out as he passed, "By

my master's brick oven, I have never seen an uglier sight than a two-headed—"

"Cease your bibble-babble, you gleeking goat's bladder!" Meggy shouted at him as she turned onto Pudding Lane.

Pudding Lane was reeky, sticky with blood that ran red in the rain, and clamorous with the cries of animals on the way to becoming chops and sausages. In front of shop after shop, carcasses of headless beasts hung from great metal hooks through their necks. Treading carefully, Meggy wabbled past the great gobs of pigs' innards that apprentices were heaving into the street. Pudding indeed, she thought.

Near halfway up Pudding Lane was a nasty, foul, and odorous shed with the simple sign RAGWORT, BUTCHER. A butcher—perhaps Ragwort himself, perhaps not—lolled in the doorway of the shop, flicking flies from his apron all beslubbered with blood. He eyed Louise greedily.

Louise hissed as if she were aware of the horrors within. "It's right sorry I am, Louise," Meggy told her, "and I shall miss you sorely.

"Good sir," Meggy called to the butcher, "I am told that the house next your shop is that of the player Cuthbert Grimm." The butcher nodded.

Roger lodged there, he had told her. Belike he would know how to save Louise. Despite Master Peevish, Meggy would not see her turned into roast goose.

~≈ SEVEN ≈~

Master Grimm's house leaned into the street, supported by half-rotted timbers and crumbling plaster. Broken windows were patched with oiled paper, and gargoyles grinned from rusted drainpipes. Players might be paid wages for pretending, Meggy thought, but it was plain they were not paid much.

She lifted the door knocker, shaped like the paw of a great iron bear, and let it drop. The door opened with a creak that startled Louise into a clamorous honking. She struggled against her restraints once more, loosed her wings from the sack, and flapped them in triumph.

"Master Grimm, Master Grimm!" shouted the woman who opened the door. "Come hither and see. There be an angel here!" Footsteps thundered, and faces popped up behind her. The woman peered closely at Meggy. "Nay, 'tis but a girl with the face of an angel, and a goose."

Meggy was surprised by the remark. Face of an angel? Had she such? No one had remarked upon it ere now. The idea pleased her, and she felt a little more assured, but still she hid her sticks in the folds of her skirt. "Is this where I might find Roger Oldham?" she asked.

"Indeed you might. You be Mistress Swann, I do expect. Come in from the rain." The faces moved back, and Meggy moved forward.

The house was crowded with people and things, sweet and sour from the smells of stewing meat, baking bread, babies' nappies, and herbs strewn on the floor.

The woman cuffed a boy aside his head. "Make haste, you, and fetch Roger," she ordered. Another boy came and helped Meggy untie Louise and put her down. A horde of children gathered and clamored about the goose.

"I be Mistress Grimm," the woman said. She was small and round, dressed in black with sleeves slashed in yellow. Her face was brown and plain as a pot but open and warm. "And here be Master Grimm and Master Merryman."

Two gentlemen stood either side of a blazing fireplace. One was round and roly-poly with a merry-looking face and several chins. The other was the bent and bony scar-faced man who had rescued Meggy in the alley. Her heart stopped its beating for a moment, alarmed again by his grotesque appearance.

The man's eyebrows rose in recognition, but he said naught about the encounter in the alley, nor did Meggy. She nodded to him and said, "Pleased to meet you, Master Grimm," for he looked grim indeed.

"Nay, nay," said Mistress Grimm. "He is Master Merryman. *This* gentleman be Master Grimm."

The smiling and nodding Master Grimm was stuffed into a doublet so tight that Meggy thought his belly might burst forth and fire buttons like cannon-shot about the room. Sparse yellow hair peeped from beneath his cap. "'Tis Dick's 'Grimm' face that has deceived you," the man said. He barked a harsh and jangly sort of laugh at his own jest and poked the other man with his elbow. "I be Cuthbert Grimm, master player. You will come to know me. All of London knows me." He pulled at his hair again and smiled a smile of self-satisfaction. Master Merryman sneered a sad sort of sneer—if, Meggy thought, a sneer might be called sad.

"Ah, Mistress Margret," Roger said, appearing at her side. "You have come to see me. Did I just see a pig fly by?"

"No nonsense, Oldmeat," Meggy said. "I am not in a sportive humor. I have come for your assistance. My father demands my goose roasted for dinner—"

Her speech was interrupted by the cries and moans of the little girls petting Louise: "You cannot cook her! You would never eat her!"

Louise looked smugly up at Roger, stretched out her long neck, and bit him on the knee.

"Hellborn goose! Fat-headed pignut! In sooth you should be roasted, you clay-brained louse!" Roger shouted, and he drew back his foot to kick her, but the children seized his leg, crying and calling to Mistress Grimm for help.

"Enough," said Mistress Grimm, pulling the girls from Roger. "I can easily put this right. Let the goose remain here with us for a time," she said to Meggy, "and find your father's dinner at a cookshop."

Louise would be saved. It was what Meggy had hoped for, but there was still a difficulty. "I have but a ha'penny," she said.

"Roger, give her coins. Fourpence, belike."

Rubbing his knee, Roger scowled and began to protest, but Mistress Grimm reached out a hand as plump as a summer melon and pinched his ear.

Roger grimaced and grinned at the same time, looking much like the gargoyles adorning the drainpipes. "Certes, with all haste, for I be always obedient to your majesty's will," he said to Mistress Grimm with a bow, and he offered Meggy some coins.

"Now," Mistress Grimm said, "all is well. Sit you down, girl, and I will fetch a mug of warm, spiced beer. You look as cold as a dead man's nose."

As Meggy sat, a swarm of little girls flew at her, asking, "For what are those sticks? Why do you walk that way? Are you wife to Roger? Where be you from? Play you games with cards? Primero, trumpit, or gleek?"

"Here, sweeting, this will warm you," Mistress Grimm said to Meggy as she returned with the mug. And to her girls, "Soft, soft, my dears. Do give the lass a chance to breathe. You remember Roger telling us of Mistress Swann with the black eyes he so admires. Dark as the plums of the blackthorn tree, he said."

Mistress Grimm and the girls all peered into Meggy's eyes as if to see for themselves. Mistress Grimm nodded, Roger blushed, and Meggy felt herself grow warm, from the beer, the compliment, and the knowledge of Roger's discomfiture.

"You, girls, move away and cease troubling Mistress Swann," Mistress Grimm said as she busied herself about the room. In her black and yellow she seemed a vast bumblebee buzzing about, straightening a bench here, patting a head there, and dropping kisses on little faces. "Stop," she shouted to the boys on the stairs. "I have told you, no dicing in here! Roger, take them upstairs and set them to learning their lines." She finally landed on a bench across from Meggy and began fanning herself with her wings—nay, her apron.

Roger herded the boys, shoving and arguing, up the stairs. The girls moved away from Meggy and then crowded around her again as she sipped the beer.

"Carter Simpson says all crooked people are witches," said a little girl with flaxen hair and dimples.

"Be you a witch?" asked another little dimpled, flaxen-haired girl.

Meggy thought to make a horrid face and shake her sticks, but the beer and the fire and the welcome had gentled her, so she simply replied, "Were I a witch, would I not cast a spell to make my legs straight and strong and turn my walking sticks into sausages?"

There was silence for a moment; then, "Belike you are right," said one.

"Carter Simpson is a dolt," said the other. "And his breath smells like the backside of a goat."

"Enough of your chatter, my girls," said Mistress Grimm. "Mistress Swann's ears are spinning."

There was silence again, but again it did not last. The tallest girl, also flaxen-haired but not dimpled, said, "I am right pleased to present myself to you, Mistress Swann. I am Violet Velvet."

"Named for Lady Ariana's ball gown in *The Revenge of Lord Gerald*. What a fine costume it was," said Mistress Grimm with a sigh.

Violet Velvet continued. "These be the twins, Ivory Silk and Silver Damask." The dimpled girls smiled at Meggy.

Meggy looked at Mistress Grimm, who obliged. "Aphrodite's and Athena's garb from the last act of *The Judgement of Paris*."

"And the boys?"

"Roger you know. The other boys are apprentices, and rascals all," she said, lifting a crawling babe onto her lap, "but this little fellow is mine. Master Grimm wanted him to be Chestnut Fustian, but I said, 'Master Grimm, if you think I will call a helpless babe Chestnut Fustian, you may think again. He will be Russet Wool.' And so he is, be you not, Russet, my love?" She cooed at him, and Meggy felt a pang, remembering long-ago cooing and cuddling. Her gran, soft and warm and smelling of meadow grasses and ale, had cooed at her so and sung her to sleep. Meggy let the little girls snuggle up against her, which eased her spirit just as the drink eased her bones.

In the sudden quiet of the room, Meggy could hear bits of conversation from the two gentlemen at the fireplace: "How know you these things . . . Thomas Bacon has left the stage and will . . . a license to play . . . noble patronage . . ."

Now the voices grew louder. "But a *bribe,* Cuthbert?" asked Master Merryman. "How have we the money for a bribe, even if we knew who and how?"

"We must do something bold," Master Grimm said.

"But will it serve us? The authorities are ever anxious to catch players in misdeeds and missteps, even when there are none."

Meggy looked quizzically at Mistress Grimm. "Another law has of late been passed against 'masterless men,'" she explained. "All players must now be licensed and attached to some noble person, lest they be taken as vagabonds, dragged before justice, whipped, stocked, burned, and packed out of the parish." She shook her head. "Fie upon it! Players, hooligans and scoundrels, discharged prisoners and landless peasants, jugglers and tinkers and horse thieves—all be treated alike."

Just then Master Grimm slammed his fist against the wall and shouted, "To treat me so—me, Cuthbert Grimm, the finest player in London. Nay, in all England! You may bow and kiss their feet if you like, you chicken-hearted coward, but I will not!"

Mistress Grimm stood, sending Russet Wool tumbling to

the floor. "I will see the gentlemen calmed. Roger," she called up the stairs, "come see your Mistress Swann home."

Roger bounced into the room. He winked at Meggy and touched his cap in agreement.

Meggy looked at Roger and then at Mistress Grimm. "You, mistress," she said, "may call me Meggy, as my gran did, if you will." Mistress Grimm nodded.

Meggy leaned down to Louise and stroked the soft whiteness of her. "Farewell, Louise. Keep out of mischief," the girl said, and then added, in a whisper, "Oh, I shall sorely feel the want of you, Louise Goose. Now I be truly alone."

Smothered with attention as she was by the little Grimms, Louise did not appear to mind being left. She blinked and preened and snapped at Roger's woolen-clad knee as he passed.

❧ EIGHT ❧

I am not your Mistress Swann, you tottering wretch," Meggy said to Roger as they started down Pudding Lane. She had to struggle to keep up with him, for, being straight and strong, he was not compelled to stick-swing-drag as she was.

"Fortunate that is for me, you mewling, flap-mouthed flax wench," he responded, slowing down a bit.

"Gleeking swag-bellied maggot," said Meggy.

"Knoddy-pated whey face."

"Fly-bitten—" The girl paused. "You have yet to say cripple-some or crookleg or leaden foot. Why do you not?"

He grinned. "When I look at you, I see not your crooked legs but your black eyes that blaze and snap and those cheeks like apples ripened in the sun," he said, which irritated but also oddly pleased the girl, which irritated her the more.

"Go to!" she snapped. "I am right surprised that you required bellows to tend your master's fire, you bloviating windbag."

Roger laughed, and Meggy found herself laughing, too. They stopped for a moment and let their laughter overtake them. Holding his side, Roger said, "You, Mistress Margret, are passing skilled at this matter of insults, you milk-livered minnow."

"I grew up in an alehouse, you wart-necked mammering clap dish."

They walked in silence for a moment through a river of garbage. Not everyone would have laughed at her insults, Meggy thought. "You be ever merry and good tempered, Old-meat," she said, "no matter if I am calling you names or Mistress Grimm is commanding you. How is that?"

Roger lifted his cap and scratched his head. "My father died when I was but twelve, and I was plucked from school and made clerk to a lawyer, who beat me fiercely on cold mornings to warm himself." He grasped Meggy's elbow and steered her clear of a mud hole one could sail a ship in. "A twelve-month of that and I ran to London. Now I do what I will and have what I will and no one beats me. Why would I not be merry?"

"Well, your sweet disposition aches my teeth, you canker blossom." Meggy stumbled over a dead dog left to rot in the street. "Fie upon this dirty city," she shouted, "home to every kind of dirt, muck, and slime God ever created."

"That may be so, but you will come to love her as I do," Roger said. "London is a fair that lasts all year. Around every corner is something wondrous—here a man with a dancing monkey, yon our good Queen Bess in silks and satins on a fine white horse. This way there's a hanging at Tyburn, that way fire eaters and rope dancers and the puppeteers in Fleet Street." Gesturing grandly, he nearly knocked Meggy into the teeming gutter.

"'Tis all here," he continued, "the fine and the ragged, the rotten and the pure. London may reek with old dirt, but her streets are filled with new hopes, new dreams, and new ideas. You are fortunate to be here, Margret Swann."

Fortunate? Meggy was unconvinced. She had ever found fortune to be fickle, false, and harsh, and belike it would be no different here in this London.

Meggy was weary and trembling with pain by the time they reached the little house on Crooked Lane. As they stopped before the door, Roger motioned toward her walking sticks. "How did it happen that you . . . that your legs . . ." He blushed. "Or am I too bold?"

"You are." He turned to walk away. "I was born so," she said to his back. "I be the most luckless person God ever did make. Or curse."

"Not so luckless," Roger said, turning toward her again. "You could also have gut griping, ruptures, catarrhs, and gravel in the back, lethargies, cold palsies, and sciatica. You might suffer from the wheezing lung or a bladder full of impost-hume or a dirt-ridden liver."

"Go to! I do not—"

"Or pustules and pimples and pocks, cankers and rashes and St. Vitus' dance."

Meggy leaned on her sticks and kicked out at him. "You are being waggish, Oldmeat," she said, "but I cannot share the humor. I cannot walk without pain, nor run, nor dance. I am called names in the street and spat upon. My mother sent me away and my father does not want me. I have nothing and no one."

"Nay, you have a friend."

"Aye, Louise, but she dwells elsewhere now."

"Not the goose. Me," he said. "Roger Oldham, at your service." With a little bow, he turned and strode away.

Meggy was struck right speechless. She opened the door to the house at the Sign of the Sun with the sense that she had left something unfinished. Something important. "Good thanks to you, Oldmeat, for seeing me home," she called after him. He lifted his cap in salute but did not turn around. "And for the coins." He lifted his cap again. "You may call me Meggy, if you will." And he lifted his cap once more.

Meggy watched him go. She had faced him with her fists up as always, but Roger had stood firm. 'Twas like poking a porridge, she thought. It did no harm to the porridge but only made her feel sticky.

As the room grew dark, Meggy wrapped herself in her cloak and lay down on her pallet. She faced a night alone, without Louise. The girl missed the warmth of the goose's body, the soft huffing of her breath, even the furious scritching and scratching after bugs in her feathers. What did Louise right now? Was she nestling with someone else? Meggy's belly prickled with loneliness, envy, and regret.

Early on the morrow, Meggy bought a roast chicken and an apple cake from a cookshop on Thames Street, hoping that Master Peevish would fail to notice that he was not eating Louise. As she returned, she saw Old Cloaks opening the stall at the front of his shop. "Damnable crookleg!" he growled, and he spat at Meggy. She thought to fling an insult at him, but then she saw a man leaving the house at the Sign of the Sun, his cloak pulled high and his hat pulled low. Not Master Peevish. A visitor? Curiosity hurried her on.

Inside, Master Peevish was sitting at the table, his head in his hands. She had seen him only three times since her arrival three days before—once he had called her a beggar, once he had paid her no heed at all, and once he had sent her from his laboratorium to the butcher's. She would speak with him now, if only she could reason out how to begin.

He looked up as the girl wabbled over to him. His peevish face was gray with fatigue, and his eyes dark shadowed. She offered him the chicken, but he waved it away.

Meggy said, "Sir, I have spent nearly all the coins that Roger gave me, and there be no food here. I will have to have money to buy more."

He gestured to the food on the table. "You have chicken."

So he knew it was not Louise, but he said naught about the goose, so neither did Meggy. "I will be hungry again tomorrow," she told him, "and every day. 'Tis how most people are."

"As fortune would have it, I have just been paid for a piece of work." Ah, Meggy wondered, did that explain the visitor? Master Peevish took a coin from a small pile on the table, gave it to Meggy, and swept the rest into his hand.

She looked at the coin on her palm. A ha'penny. "Sir," she said, "'tis but half a penny and not worth very much. It will take more to buy bread and cheese and mayhap apples. And candles, for 'tis monstrous dark in here. And—"

Frowning, he dropped more coins onto the table, stood up, and headed for the stairs.

"Sir," Meggy called after him, "what do I here? Why did you send for me? What shall I be about?"

He turned and looked at her. "Might your legs withstand a trip to the inn at the top of the lane? I would have a pail of ale . . . err, mistress."

"Margret," Meggy said, but he was gone up the stairs. She bit her lip in disappointment. It appeared that her speech with him would have to wait.

She wabbled up the lane and back down with a pail of ale over her arm, walking very, very slowly lest she spill and tipsify the ground and not Master Peevish. Who was the visitor? What work had Master Peevish done? Was he near to finding what he sought? Might he truly transform things and make them perfect, as Roger had said? She was doubtful. More likely 'twas but the foolish fancy of the peevish man in the faded black gown.

Her legs ached from walking and her head from wondering by the time she returned to the house at the Sign of the Sun. The window and door of the cooper's shop were thrown open, revealing inside a tangle of wood planks, tools, and barrel staves. The cooper's boy sat in a drift of sawdust and wood chips, playing with his horse, while the cooper smoothed the sides of a barrel. Sawdust flew around their heads.

Meggy laughed. "It appears to be snowing wood, Master Cooper," she said. The cooper grinned and saluted her with his smoothing tool.

Had she made a friend? In truth, another friend—for Roger called himself such. Two friends who were not geese. She had ne'er bethought her that such a thing would happen. I know I did swear I needed no friend but Louise, she said to herself, but I feel like the sun is shining inside me.

Of a sudden there was a loud crack from inside the house at the Sign of the Sun. Ye toads and vipers! Meggy hastened in, the pail of ale strewing golden drops as she let it fall to the floor. Up the stairs she went as fast as she was able.

The laboratorium was filled with smoke, out of which appeared Master Peevish, his face all sooty and black except for where the caterpillars were burned clear off his brow.

"Sir," she began, "are you—" But he waved her silent.

"I have unfortunately discovered three elements one should not heat together," he said. "I must make note of this." From the shelf he took a large book marked with sooty fingerprints and globs of candle wax, opened it, and began to write.

Meggy lumbered back downstairs and mopped up what ale had spilled with the hem of her kirtle. She sat down at the table and feasted on chicken and apple cake. The bemadding man, she thought. Next time it might be his head he loses and not just his eyebrows.

She finished eating and threw the chicken bones into the street. She sat again. And stood again. She was wearied with looking at the walls of the poky, cramped, little house. How small was it? She measured steps from side to side—but six paces across. A house this tiny belike was better suited to an elf, she thought, and she sang:

> *And a little elf man, elf man, elf man,*
> *And a little elf man said unto me,*
> *Come and nurse an elf child, elf child, elf child,*
> *Come and nurse an elf child down beneath the sea.*

An elf child, yes, an elf child would be at home in this bawbling little house. She would need a wee cradle, a drinking cup, and a plate. Made of a leaf and an acorn, belike, and a piece of spider web for a coverlet . . . Ye toads and vipers, Meggy thought, mark me. I sound right daft.

She was lonely, she realized, and weary of singing and pretending and worrying in the little room downstairs. All that happens in this house happens up in that smoky chamber, she thought. Vexed, restless, and curious as a cat at a mousehole, she climbed upstairs, dragging the pail of ale up stair by stair behind her.

The alchemist was unstopping a large vial of a green liquid when she entered the laboratorium. "Sir," she said, "prithee, Master Peev—err, Ambrose, I would speak with you."

He kept his eyes on the liquid bubbling in a long-necked vessel and said naught.

She went closer to him. He did not look up. "Sir!" she said loudly.

He jumped like a frog in a thunderstorm.

"Sir," she said again, "pray pardon my interruption, but I am grown sore tired of sitting downstairs. You sent for me and here I am. I beg you give me some task to do."

Master Ambrose looked at Meggy as if a fish had spoken to him, but she went on. "I am not a son, but I am able and willing to learn. Mayhap I could assist you in your laboratorium? I might wash vessels and scrub pots and"—she looked around the room—"work the bellows to make the fire hot. I have grown more knowing about the streets of London now, so I can find what you require for your work and carry it back in my sack, if it is not too heavy or cumbersome, if I do not have to walk too far, if you do not need it straightway, for I am not swift—"

The man held up his hand to silence her. He looked at her closely, and his brow, where the caterpillars had once capered, furled. "Mayhap you could be somewhat useful . . . err, mistress . . ."

"Margret," Meggy said.

NINE

R oger had not come again to the house at the Sign of the Sun. Although Meggy missed his company and his teasing, she had no good reason to seek him out at his lodgings at the house of Cuthbert Grimm. Sometimes she thought she saw him in the street, and she smiled, but so far her sightings were not Roger but some peddler or wherryman or tall young fellow with fine shoulders.

So, as the summer days passed, Meggy lessened her loneliness by assisting the alchemist in the laboratorium. She polished the tongs and pumped the bellows, washed vessels of glass and earthenware, arranged shelves of long-handled spoons and short-necked bottles. She puzzled out how to carry the buckets of water upstairs—bucket up one step, Meggy and her sticks up, bucket up another step, over and over. Step by step, the same way, she took the empty buckets back down for the water bearer.

Master Peevish worked in a silence broken only by bubbling and dripping. Meggy watched him closely, and her curiosity grew until one day it burbled out of her: "Be there gold yet in that cup? I see nothing but black powder. How will—"

"The Devil take you!" the alchemist shouted. "I cannot work with you buzzing like a gnat in my ear."

Meggy's knees trembled a little, but she made certain her voice did not as she challenged him. "Were you to tell me what you are doing and why, belike I would not have so very many questions."

He glared at her. "Roger did not ask to know the why or wherefore."

"Roger cares only for playing," she said, "but I would know." Meggy waited in fearful silence for the man's reaction to her boldness.

Master Ambrose pulled on his earlobe, once, twice, three times, and finally said, "In words even you might comprehend, I seek to break apart by art things combined by nature, to transform and purify them until I have a substance so pure, it can purify other matter." He paced in his enthusiasm from wall to window and back. "This substance, called the elixir of life or the fifth essence or the philosopher's stone, when cast upon the imperfect will perfect it. 'Tis this elixir I seek."

"Go to! This is true? And it will make gold?"

"Making gold is but a step in the process of transformation," he said, and he pulled a book down off the shelf. "Base metal is an imperfect or diseased state of gold, the perfect metal. When I discover the means of transforming base metal into gold, I can apply that method to other substances, even living things, and perfect them in their nature."

Master Ambrose consulted his book and nodded. He then poured gray crystals into a crucible and set Meggy to stirring them with a long-handled spoon.

"Can you now transform things?" she asked him.

"Oh, aye, solids into liquids, liquids into vapors. But in time all the secrets of transformation will be known to me."

"And then you will make gold?"

"More than that. The Arab Jabir says that one thousand fusions will change gold into the elixir of life. Once I have that, I will have the means of transforming humans into perfect, immortal beings. Eternal youth. Immortality. That is my Great Work. The man who has the secret of immortality will have riches and power beyond dreams." He began to work the bellows to make the fire hotter as Meggy continued her stirring. "Great men throughout time have said it can be done," he said, breathless from pumping. "Aristotle, Paracelsus, Albertus Magnus, Thomas Aquinas, Roger Bacon . . ."

And you? Meggy wondered. Great men, perhaps, but likely not tall, peevish, shabby men with burnt eyebrows. She shook her head.

The alchemist lifted the bellows like a sword. "Think of it, err, mistress," he said. "Immortality. Eternal life."

Meggy stopped her stirring. "I have found that living can be most toilsome and cruel. Why would any someone wish to be immortal?"

"The queen herself, it is said, will reward handsomely the man who brings her the secret." He took the spoon from Meggy and handed her the bellows. "Enough of your prattle. Cease your drumbling, take these bellows, and encourage these flames."

For many days Meggy pumped the bellows, added coal to the fire, and tended the alembic, the glass instrument that turned liquid into vapor and back again. This Great Work of his takes a goodly long time, she thought as she ground sal ammoniac in a mortar and heated sulfur and alum in a crucible until it was reduced to a powder. When the man's work did not go well, he threw pots against the wall or swept objects off the shelves with his long arms, and Meggy spent a fair amount of time straightening bottles and jars and righting candles. He called her "err, mistress," although she always replied, "I am Margret, sir."

Slowly the alchemist and the girl grew accustomed to one another, and she once again dared to interrupt with questions she had been pondering. "How, sir," she asked him, "can one make one metal into another? Is not a thing what it is and it cannot be another thing? Is it not as God made it and none other?"

He sighed and marked a place in his book with his finger. "All substances are composed of the same matter," he said. "Their differences are due to the presence of different qualities imposed upon them, such as redness or hardness or coldness. By taking away those qualities, I hope to isolate the prime material of a substance, and then, by adding other qualities, to transform its very essence."

Meggy's brain swirled. "Just what is that you say?"

He pulled at his earlobe once, twice, three times before continuing, "It is simple. Add cold, and water turns to ice. Heat it, and it becomes water again. In the kitchen raw dough turns to bread when heat is applied." He gestured to a bottle of red powder. "So too does cinnabar change. Heated, it turns to mercury, a silver liquid. If I could discover how to remove the liquidity from the mercury, it would harden and become silver."

"And how would that make a person immortal?"

"It would be a step, err, mistress. Silver could then be transformed to gold, and gold is the perfection of metal. So too is immortality the perfection of life. With every experiment, I make progress and am closer to what I seek."

Meggy remained unpersuaded, but over the days she saw small transformations. Dark, brittle flakes of metal were turned into vapor by heating and were made solid again by cooling. She boiled water until naught remained but a fine grit; the water had turned into earth, the master said. She watched as heat applied to the red powdered cinnabar produced silver mercury, just as he had told her, and yellow powdered sulfur turned black. Master Peevish looked less peevish when his mixing and measuring gave him the results he wanted. "Now, by my faith, this is a most welcome surprise," he said as a heated metal released white solids and red smoke. And "'Tis wondrous, is't not?" when a powdered gray substance began to glow.

Meggy saw naught she thought perfect or immortal or gold, but she continued to help in the laboratorium, where at least she was warm and occupied and not alone.

Each day the master sent Meggy for salt, for sulfur, for something. She was most slow at these errands and often had to stop and rest, but he did not remark, nor perhaps even notice, her lagging. If he remembered to give the girl coins to pay for provisions, she used a penny or two to buy bread or sausage or apples, for he gave little thought to food, so engaged was he in his Great Work. The food she took him often dried and spoiled in the heat of the laboratorium, and Meggy added it to the river of refuse in the street.

To her surprise, mighty London proved small and cramped. Hither to yon, wall to wall, was but a short distance, shorter than the distance from her mother's alehouse to the river. Even so, her hands grew rough and sore from holding the sticks. Her arms ached, and her legs, but the busy and colorful London streets often diverted her. The city was a minglement of great houses next to small, shops next to gardens, churches by stables and kennels by inns. Ballad sellers sang, hawkers hawked, horses and carts and coaches hurried by. A hodgepodge it was, a hurly-burly, but she began to grow accustomed to the crowds and the refuse and the reeky gutters.

Sitting by the warm furnace working the bellows, she often found herself singing the ballads she had learned from her gran. And that is what she was about one day when church bells began their clangor.

"Is't midday already?" Master Ambrose asked, wiping his hands on his gown. "Hie you to the apothecary for a measure of antimony."

"Anon, sir, I be—"

"Now," he said. "Quick away."

She stood. "Master Wormwood says you are a man of skill and vision, but he will extend no more credit, for we are exceedingly in his debt. 'Pence,' quoth he, 'not promises.'"

Master Ambrose huffed and gestured to a shelf by the door. "Take coins from yon copper pot and give them to the thieving Wormwood, that penny-pinching nipcheese, and remind him there be other apothecaries in London."

"Methinks they all prefer pence to promises," Meggy said, putting down the bellows and picking up her walking sticks.

Outside she took a deep breath. Although the late-summer days were still warm, autumn was nigh. Her village would be scented with wood fires and ripening apples. Would there be such pleasant smells here, or just the stench of the city gutters? she wondered as she watched young ravens picking at rib bones in a gutter. She sang softly: *There were three ravens sat on a tree, Downe a downe, hay downe hay downe, They were as black as they might be, With a downe derrie der—*

Ye toads and vipers. She had forgotten the coins.

She wabbled back down the lane and into the house, and

made her slow and painful way up the stairs. Breathless, she stopped before the door.

There were voices in the laboratorium. Master Peevish had visitors. He never had visitors. Then she recalled the shadowy figures creeping in and out of the house while she tried to sleep.

She did not think he would welcome an interruption. Mayhap if she opened the door a crack and leaned in to reach the coins in the pot . . .

"I have given you my word," Master Ambrose was saying. "I have naught left of any value but my work and my word." Meggy marked that he did not add "and my daughter."

She opened the door a bit wider and stretched her arm longer, almost, almost to the pot. Peering through the crack, she beheld a man with a wild mop of orange hair pacing about the little room. "The baron be ever more powerful each day," the man said. "Should he be named to the privy council, 'twill mean an end to us. This matter must be dispatched with all haste."

Someone else, someone she could not see, said, "I must taste every dish he partakes of, and I have no wish to depart this earth before my time. Good sir, can you assure my life?"

"I have no small reputation, sirrah," said the alchemist. "Be not afeared. Your tolerance to the substance will grow from doses in wine each day, and when the fatal dose be added to his food, you will merely sicken. Many times I have done this, and I do know what I am about."

Fatal dose? Master Peevish pursued something fatal . . . did that not mean deadly? And he had done it afore? Oh ye toads and vipers. Was this the abracadabra Master Old Cloaks had meant? Would she see the alchemist in the Tower? Or worse, would the hair of his severed head blow in the breeze on London Bridge? She shivered, and one of her sticks clattered to the floor.

The ginger-haired man hurried to the door, grabbed Meggy's arm, and pulled her through, pinning her stick down with his foot. He had small, piggish eyes in an ill-humored face. There seemed a dark, wet smell about him that affrighted her. "Who or what is this?" he hissed.

"No one of account," Master Ambrose said. And to Meggy he added, "Err, mistress, err, begone."

Meggy was indeed eager to be gone, but the other man, fat paunched and pale, said, "She cannot go. She has heard us."

The pig-eyed man sneered and pushed Meggy away. "She be naught but an accursed cripple. I do wager her wits are as misshapen as her limbs."

"Aye," the alchemist said, coming to her side. He picked up her fallen stick and handed it to her. "That is the way of her. She be but a moonling, hearing little and understanding less. Go," he said loudly. And then he whispered, "Make haste. Away!"

Meggy went. She went as swiftly as a person with misshapen limbs and wits could go. And her heart pounded as she hurried from the house.

❧ T E N ❧

The antimony forgotten, Meggy waited until the men, and then her father, had left the house before she returned. The girl pondered through a restless night. The alchemist had rescued her from those villains, but what was he doing with them at all?

In the morning she climbed again to the laboratorium. "Sir," she said, "about what I heard—"

"You heard naught, mistress," the alchemist responded.

"But you said—"

"I said naught. Naught."

She prayed she had merely misunderstood, that her robustious imagination had caused these fancies of poison and death. She looked at Master Peevish, who was bent over a book, turning the pages with sooty fingers. Were those the hands of a murderer? His face was moody and troubled, not murderous. But her fear did not vanish, merely shriveled into a tiny, uncomfortable knot.

Heating glass and clay vessels was a treacherous business. They often cracked or shattered. That day Master Ambrose showed her how to prepare a cement for mending the repairable breaks—old cheese, roots, pitch, boiled horses' hooves, and turpentine. Boiled all together, they emitted a stench so horrendous, Meggy thought she would heave her gorge as she stirred, but she did not and was rewarded with a nod.

The sun was high in the sky when the master said, "Mistress, err, mistress, I wish you to go to Master Pomfret's shop, in the alley off Paul's Chain at the west end of the city. Tell him I require a worm condenser."

"Aye, certes," she said. "What is a worm condenser?"

"You need not concern yourself. Master Pomfret knows."

The alchemist described the quickest way to Paul's Chain, and Meggy, her sack over her shoulder, set off. A warm, dry, gritty wind blew her west along Candlewick Street, and then Budge Row, with its lamb skinners and fur merchants. Blue-coated apprentices called copper pots and silver knives. Peddlers offered oysters, meat pies, cesspit cleaning. Vendors balanced baskets of produce on their heads or carried open pails of fly-speckled milk for sale.

Beggars grabbed and shoved and howled their misery. One of them screeched to another, "Leave my corner, you wart-necked, flap-mouthed maggot!" and Meggy remembered trading insults with Roger so many weeks ago. What did the boy now? Was he busy with his playmaking? Was that why he did not come to see her? Had he forgotten his pledge of friendship?

She walked on. Some streets were wider and houses larger, and there she saw shops offering fur-trimmed cloaks and leather-bound books; compasses and drinking goblets of silver and gold; coifs, gorgets, sleeves, and ruffs for the fashionable. Men in richly furred robes and gold chains passed by, and fine ladies with pomanders held to their noses. A man with a ruff so big it looked like he carried his head on a platter gave Meggy a merry laugh until, with a shiver, she remembered the heads on London Bridge.

The sun shone more fiercely and the day grew hot. Meggy stopped a moment to cool her head, rest her aching legs, and ease her sore hands. "Come and buy the latest ballad," said a ballad seller suddenly beside her. "'Antiprognostication,' it is called, an invective against the vain and unprofitable predictions of astrologers. Or this epitaph upon the death of . . ." He took a closer look at Meggy and said, "Belike not that one for a fair young mistress. Here be a tale of romance and betrayal: *Young Johnstone and the young colonel sat drinking at the wine*," the ballad seller sang. "*Oh if ye would marry my sister, then I would marry thine.*"

Meggy shook her head. "'Tis a fine story, but I have no pennies to spend." The ballad seller shrugged and turned away, but Meggy did have a question. She pulled at his sleeve and pointed to the great building with spires and towers she had seen ahead of her for some while. "Be that the queen's palace?"

"Nay, mistress, 'tis Paul's, the greatest church in Christendom," said the ballad seller. "Know you not St. Paul's?"

St. Paul's seemed more a small city than a church. Houses and shops bordered the churchyard. Meggy passed the barbershop of one Master Tiffin, a button shop even smaller than her own small house, and stalls selling pins, pens, and paper.

Inside the yard was the great church, with its charred and broken steeple, vast covered galleries, an outdoor pulpit with roof and a cross atop, and centuries of grave markers. Bookshops and stalls clustered along the walls and at the doors of the church itself. She peeped into windows of establishments marked with the signs of the Brazen Serpent and the Green Dragon, the White Lion, the Queen's Arms, and the Blazing Star, betokening bookshops teeming with news sheets and broadsides, printed books, hornbooks for children, and illustrations of hair-raising wonders.

The street called Paul's Chain boasted large houses and shops, but in the alley the shops were smaller, the street narrower and dirtier, and the crowds less. Even on this warm day it was gloomy and dank, pitted with mud holes where garbage and fresh sewage puddled.

The shutters were open on a tiny shop with an even tinier stall in front. Ballads and other broadsides were pasted on every surface and lined its shelves.

She peeked inside, where there were more shelves crowded with stacks of paper, boxes, racks, and mysterious stuffed leather bags on the ends of sticks, the purpose of which Meggy could not imagine, unless they were for small boys to beat each other with.

And in the center of the shop was a wooden table topped with a great levered screw. It looked to Meggy to be an instrument of torture, likely to press a man into a shadow and squeeze the vinegar right out of him. "I do believe it a fiendish device for punishment," she said aloud.

"Nay, 'tis a hand press, for printing," said a man come out of the shop with his hands full of papers. "Writing without a pen—or perhaps with many pens at once."

"Go to! Be you a wizard?" she asked.

He smiled. "Nay, mistress, merely the printer. Do you wish to buy a ballad? Or to have one printed?"

Meggy shook her head. "I am but passing on my way to Master Pomfret's."

"In faith, you have not heard? Master Pomfret died a sevennight ago and was carried toes up to the churchyard at Paul's."

"Ye toads and vipers!" said Meggy, pushing her hair back from her damp, hot face. "Then I am come all this way for naught."

"Come in and rest a moment," the printer said, "afore making your journey back. And we might find some cool ale to share. I have no business that cannot wait."

Meggy nodded her thanks, and a question bubbled up. "Why are you here and not with the houses and shops nearer St. Paul's, which are finer and crowded with customers?"

"I would wish to be at Paul's, where business is better and customers richer, but shops be cheaper here."

Meggy looked about her at the dark and muddy street, the sagging houses, and the puddles of slop and rubbish. "I doubt not that it is cheaper," she said. "'Tis a wonder people are not paid to live here."

The printer barked a laugh as he showed Meggy into the shop and pulled up a stool for her. At that moment a child toddled over. Lifting the wee girl into the air, the printer said, "This is my Gilly. Is she not fine? Have you ever seen a more splendid child than my Gillyflower?" He bent his head and blew kisses in her neck, which made the child wriggle and laugh.

Meggy felt a stab of sadness and envy. This is a father, she thought. Master Peevish had never touched her and certainly did not think her splendid. He did not even know her name.

Gilly swung her strong, sturdy legs in delight. Meggy remembered being that young, but crooked and in pain. She felt a touch of pity and tenderness for the lame little Meggy she had once been. She reached out to tickle Gilly's bare toes and was rewarded with a tiny laugh. "Do you like ginger cakes?" Meggy asked the girl.

Gilly stuffed most of her little fist into her mouth and nodded.

"Next penny I have to spend, I shall spend on ginger cakes and bring you one."

Gilly took her hand from her mouth and with it, all sticky and wet, touched Meggy's cheek.

Meggy wabbled home empty-handed, aching and tired but feeling warm inside from the printer's kindness and Gilly's touch. The warmth survived even Master Peevish's displeasure at the loss of Master Pomfret and the mysterious worm condenser.

After such a day, Meggy slept deeply, dreaming of ballad sellers, sticky babies, and heads on platters. Near dawn her dreams turned to smoked sausages and hams, and she awoke to the smell of fire. Pulling on her bodice and kirtle and wrapping her cloak around her, she threw the door open and hurried into the street.

The doors and windows of the cooper's shop were open wide, and she could see stacks of wood and piles of shavings ablaze. The barrel staves were small towers of flame. Two men of the watch pulled a wagon laden with leather buckets of water up to the shop, and they, the cooper, and two drunken gentlemen in stained padded doublets poured water onto the floor and splashed it on the walls.

Neighborers, some still in nightclothes and bare feet, hastened from their houses and shops to help, pouring jugs of water on the hot coals and beating at the flames with wet burlap sacks. But not her father, Meggy marked. Had he not heard the commotion?

The morning was cool and dewy, and the fire soon slowed into steaming and smoldering. The walls still stood, the room above was still covered by the roof, but inside the shop all was ash, scraps, and debris.

The cooper crossed to where his son waited. "Charger was sleeping down here. Where is he?" the boy asked.

His father took his hand. "Gone, boy. Your horse, the finished barrels, my stock of wood, most of the staircase . . . gone." His voice dwindled as the boy broke into sobs he tried to muffle but could not.

Master Old Cloaks watched from the shadows. After a moment he crossed over to the cooper and, pointing to Meggy, said, "It be that one, her, the Devil's spawn, the cursed cripple, who fired your shop, Master Cooper. It be that one, the daughter of the adept of the black arts. See how her house was spared. Next it will be my shop afire and then yours," he said to the neighborers standing by, "if we do not stop her." Shivers prickled Meggy's spine like icy water dripping from the eaves, and she began to back slowly toward her door.

Everyone fell silent. There was no sound but for the crackling of sparks and hissing of embers. The cooper looked at Master Old Cloaks and then at Meggy. The watchmen and the neighborers watched them both, and then the cooper spoke. "Nay," he said, "the fire had naught to do with her. My son but dropped a candle in the night, and the shavings quickly caught."

"I say it was her doing," Master Old Cloaks said. "See her affliction. See how she is marked by the Devil."

Meggy's heart thumped with fright, but the taller watchman grabbed Master Old Cloaks and said, "You are ever a troublemaker, with your annoyous curses and your accusations, your gripes and grouses. Begone from here afore I take you in for spreading slander."

Grumbling, Master Old Cloaks retreated, still casting spiteful glances at Meggy. The watchman nodded to her. In the growing light of day, she saw his cheek, disfigured by a large red birthmark of the kind that is called a witch's mark. Belike he too had been shouted at and spat upon in the streets, Meggy thought. She smiled her thanks.

The watchman nodded again as he picked up his lantern, bell, and staff and followed his partner down Crooked Lane. The tipsy gentlemen returned to their drink, and the others, grateful that their homes were spared, drifted away to break the night's fast with warm bread and cool ale.

The cooper's shop still smoked and smoldered. "When it has cooled a bit," Meggy heard the cooper say to his son, "we will search for what remains."

"And we will find Charger?" asked the boy again.

"No, belike Charger is gone."

Meggy returned to the house at the Sign of the Sun. The day was growing lighter. She sat herself at the table and chewed a piece of yesterday's bread. Her heart finally slowed its thumping, but her thoughts raced. When she heard Master Peevish's footsteps above, she climbed the stairs to the laboratorium, carrying a piece of bread for him.

"Ah, mistress . . . err, mistress, well met," he said. "I have a task for—"

"Sir, there was a fire in the cooper's shop," she said as she handed him the bread, "and all the neighborers came to help. Did you not hear the hubbub or smell the smoke?"

"I was at my work," he said. "Come hither—I require your assistance. Pour this solution into—"

"Soft, sir, soft. First I require yours," Meggy said. "The man at the old cloak shop next us curses and spits at me in the street."

"What care I what the man does?"

"He wishes me ill. This very morning he did accuse me of setting the fire in the cooper's shop. I pray you speak to him ere he—"

"Fie upon it!" Master Ambrose shouted, waving his bread. "Do not bother me with trifles. Now take this—"

Meggy's cheeks flamed. "Anon, sir," she said. "I do think this matter no trifle and must attend to it without delay." She picked up her walking sticks, wabbled to the door, and started down the stairs. A cold selfish man, he was, she thought. A mean, small, petty, and ungenerous man who could not stir himself to help her—or anyone. It appears I must strain the curdle from this custard myself, she thought.

She sat down at the table, chin in her hand. If only, she thought, she could drive Old Cloaks off with threats of the Devil and the evil eye as she had the children in her village. She opened her eyes wider. Aye, she thought, aye, that might serve. And she left the house, her hands trembling on the walking sticks in anger and fear and excitement, as she wabbled to the shop of Master Old Cloaks.

He frowned when he saw her and might have spat, but she spoke first. "I wish to strike a bargain with you," she said. "If you cease shouting and spitting and hurling accusations at me, I will not fire your shop."

He looked about at the piles of old cloaks and doublets and shoes, and his face grew pale. Even so he took a step toward her and said, "I do not bargain with detestable crooklegs and Devil's spawn."

"As you will," said Meggy. "I shall call upon my legion of demons to assist me in my dark work. Belike we will begin by burning this row of fine leather boots." She motioned to him. "It were best you stand apart, lest you be scorched by the flames."

The man's mouth gaped and his eyes bulged. "Nay, nay!" he shouted. "I will do as you wish. Avaunt! Aroint, you witch! Leave my shop and take your fiends, demons, and hobgoblins with you."

Thundering toads, the lean-witted old goat truly believes I can do it, Meggy thought. He was more gullible and more craven than even the youngest villager! Never had her affliction served her so well. "We will leave you in peace," she said, "all of us, so long as you remember our bargain. You, little imp, hiding in the corner. Pick up your tail and come along. Yes, that is right."

Staring at the corner, Master Old Cloaks flattened himself against the wall. "We give you good morrow, sir," Meggy called over her shoulder as she left the shop.

Once safely back in the house at the Sign of the Sun, Meggy let her breath out with a whoosh. She dropped onto the bench and rested her head on the table. Belike it was dangerous, her pretending to be a witch, but she thought the watchman's threats would keep Master Old Cloaks silent. And Roger should have seen me, she thought. He would doubt not what a fine player I would be. Relief, pride, and amazement at what she had done with her poor pennyworth of courage filled her.

Master Peevish hastened down the stairs and through the room. Meggy sat up. "Sir, I am returned," she began, but he waved her off.

"I must away," he said, and he hastened out the door and up Crooked Lane.

Meggy was hungry. She climbed to the laboratorium and looked for coins in the copper pot. There were not many, and none were gold. Meggy snorted as she fished them out. Great Work indeed. Immortality, hmph. Better he should seek to change metal into sausages so she could eat.

In a cookshop on Thames Street Meggy bought a rabbit pie and a berry tart. On arriving back at the house at the Sign of the Sun, she climbed again to the laboratorium, where she left half the pie for her father. She tucked one penny into her bodice, for she knew she would be hungry again anon, and put the remaining coins back into the copper pot.

She ate a bit of the rabbit pie but finished every crumb of the berry tart, sitting on her pallet before the empty fireplace, delighting in the juicy sweetness that ran down her chin.

⟨ E L E V E N ⟩

When he returned, Master Peevish spurned her help, so Meggy went to see how the cooper fared. His shop smoked but still stood. Inside, the cooper was sifting through the soggy ashes of his planks and barrels.

"Right sorry I am for your trouble, Master Cooper," Meggy said from the doorway.

He smiled a weak smile and said, "I thank you for your kind thoughts, Mistress Meggy, but the fire has burned out, my stock can be replaced, and, God grant us mercy, my son is safe. Our troubles be trifling indeed."

The cooper's son came to her side, wiping tears from his soot-streaked face. "My horse is gone," he said to her, "and I like not all these reeky ashes."

The cooper pulled at his hair until it stood up on his head like tufts of red grass. "I told you, boy, you must—"

In the smoky air Meggy saw her granny's face. What Gran would do is what I shall do, she thought, and she took the boy's hand. "He must come and listen to a ballad, that is what he must. It be a right good story, and I am eager to share it."

The girl sat on the doorstep in the only spot of sunshine that found its way into Crooked Lane. Nicholas sat beside her and wiped his nose on his sleeve.

"So, listen with patient ears, young Master Nicholas," Meggy said, "and I will begin the tale of the strange wedding of a frog and a mouse."

"What kind of mouse?" he asked, wiping his nose on his other sleeve.

"An ordinary mouse. Gray and small. With a tail. Runs about in the meadow."

"What kind of meadow?"

"A meadow, a green meadow, a brown meadow, any meadow. Now hearken." And she began to sing, as her gran had, not so many years ago:

> *A frog he would a-wooing go,*
> *A-too-re-lal, a-too-re-lal,*
> *He went into Miss Mousie's hall,*
> *A-too-re-lal, a-too-re-lal*

"What means *a-too-re—*"

Meggy pinched the boy's lips together gently. "Hush. You tire out your tongue and my ears, Master Gibble Gabble." Nicholas sat at Meggy's side and listened until she arrived at, *The frog came swimming cross the lake, and there got swallowed by a snake, a-too, ad-diddle-de-day.*

"Why did the snake eat him?"

"Belike frogs look all good and juicy to a snake, as joints of beef and legs of chicken and roasted pork ribs look to us." Meggy's belly rumbled at the picture.

"Why?" Nicholas squeaked.

Meggy sighed a great sigh and leaned back against the front of the building, where the wood was warm from the sun. "Enough of your annoyous prattle. You have more questions than I have answers."

"Sing me a story about a horse," Nicholas said.

Before she could respond, the cooper came out with bread and a bit of cold sausage, which he gave to Meggy. "Nicholas and I must to Cooper's Hall to discover what aid the guild might offer. My thanks to you for attending the boy. Since his mother died, he lacks a woman's care."

Meggy had enjoyed the sun, the singing, and the warm, small-child smell of Nicholas. Now, as she finished her sausage, she thought again of her promise to take a ginger cake to Gilly, the printer's girl.

Meggy stood, brushed crumbs from her bodice, and climbed to Eastcheap, where she spent her penny on two ginger cakes. One she ate right there in the food shop, licking her fingers so as to savor every crumb. The other she carried across London to the printer's.

The printer was standing in the doorway of his shop when Meggy arrived. "What lack you, mistress? See a new broadside come forth. Buy a new ballad for—" He stopped when he recognized her. "A good morrow to you, little mistress," he said.

"Good day, Master Printer. I be Margret Swann, but you may call me Meggy, as my gran did."

"Well met, Meggy Swann. And I be John Allyn, impoverished printer," he said with a little bow.

Meggy looked past him into the shop, at the great levered contraption he had called a hand press, the compartmented boxes, sticks, racks, and mysterious stuffed leather bags. "Are all these objects used for printing?" she asked.

"Indeed. Come inside and I will show you."

"I have brought a ginger cake for Gilly," she said.

"Nay," said the printer, pulling up a stool for her, "you should not have come all this way for that. You are not strong enough nor hearty—"

Frowning, Meggy waved away his pity and his stool. "I will stand, Master Printer. I am not breakable, and I be stronger than I look." And to her surprise she realized she was.

"Ah, here is my Gillyflower, who should be napping," said the printer as the little girl toddled out. Meggy wabbled toward her, but Gilly, affrighted, ran to her father and held tightly to the hem of his jerkin.

"Do not be afraid, Gilly," Meggy said. "I may be crooked, but I come with the freshest, sweetest ginger cake in all of London." She held out the cake, and slowly Gilly let go her father, took the cake from Meggy with a small smile, and scampered off to the back of the shop.

"Deftly done, mistress," said Master Allyn to Meggy, who found she took pleasure in making children smile. "Now you shall see how ballads come forth." The printer moved to the press, laid a piece of paper over the tray, grasped the lever, and leaned forward, so that the screw pushed the whole top of the press down against the paper. When he pulled the handle up and removed the paper, there were letters on the page. Nay, words. An entire page of words!

Meggy could hardly breathe with the wonder of it. Here was true abracadabra. "Is it magic?" she asked.

"Not a bit. Printing, it is," Master Allyn said, "writing by means of a machine."

"Wondrous," Meggy said, "'tis a wondrous machine."

"Aye. But 'tis wasteful that I use it only to print ballad sheets and broadsides for impecunious poets."

"Might you not print other things?"

"The queen has given preference to so many printers— John Day may print ABCs and catechisms; Jugge prints Bibles; Tottle, law books; Roberts and Watkins, almanacs and prognostications, and so forth—that there is not much left for the rest of us."

"I have fine imaginings and I know a great many words," Meggy said. "Mayhap I could write something for you to print. But I cannot pay."

He laughed. "Yet another impecunious poet. I vow, I am infested with them." He took the printed page and draped it over a rod to dry. "I have trade aplenty, which means I have no time, but still no money. How that happens is a mystery. Ah," he said, turning, "here are Mistress Allyn and young Robert."

A young woman, carrying a baby in her arms and another,

it appeared, in her belly, came into the shop. She handed the baby to Master Allyn. "Eustace Price," she said, "will be here on the morrow with an epitaph on the death of Umphrey Spenser that he wishes printed. And Andrew Gypkin wants us to print his broadside condemning broadsides." She laughed. "He says they promote scandal and smut and debauchery."

"He yet owes me for the ballad warning London women against the sin of vanity," Master Allyn said. "Did he speak to you of payment?"

"He says you will be paid by selling them." She held her great belly with one arm as she leaned against the wall.

Gilly called from back of the shop, "Papa, come—I have wet me."

Master Allyn sighed. "Sell? When have I time to stroll the streets to sell sheets of Gypkin's rantings?"

Meggy bade them farewell, left them to their troubles, and went home to her own.

Her father was seated at the table, a jug of ale before him. He looked up at her, his eyes as flat and black and cold as bits of coal in his pale face. "Behold, daughter," he said, his voice slow and thick. Cupshot, Meggy thought. She knew the signs. "See what my Great Work has brought me to." He took a mighty swallow.

What meant he? Was he speaking of the men she had seen in the laboratorium?

Meggy sat down across from him. "My daughter," he said, shaking his head. "Your mother . . . is she well?"

Meggy was astonished. Ne'er had he mentioned her mother. The girl nodded; her mother was no doubt well . . . she always was.

"Be she yet the most beauteous woman in the county?"

Beauteous she was, but how best to describe her? "She is as beauteous as ice crystals on a windowpane, as water rumbling over rocks, as bolts of lightning shooting cross a darkened sky."

The alchemist nodded. "In sooth Bess was ne'er easy," he said, "but a beauty nonetheless."

Ne'er easy? A kindly thing to say. Meggy herself thought her mother as bad tempered as a wet witch.

The man inspected the girl. "You have not the look of her."

"I believe I have the look of you, sir," Meggy said, surprised that it was true, "for we share the same dark hair and lean-fleshed form."

"But your lameness," he said, gesturing, "whence is that?"

Meggy was surprised that he cared enough to ask. "My gran said I was born this way and never did learn to walk right. My mother told me it was God's curse on me."

He shook his head. "Nonsense. Village ignorance."

Nonsense? Ignorance? This conversation was full of surprises, Meggy thought. Perhaps, full of ale as he was, he might talk of other things that she had long wanted to know. She refilled his mug from the jug on the table.

"Sir," she began. She cleared her throat. "Sir, if you please, wilt say how you happened upon my mother and how I came to be?"

He took a large swallow of his ale and wiped his lips on his sleeve. For long moments he sat in silence, and then he said, "I was at Oxford and it was spring. Inspired by the great Paracelsus, I desired to know man not through books but by knowing his world, so I took to the road. My travels sent me south, through London, to Millford village, where I stopped for refreshment at an alehouse." He nodded at Meggy. "An alehouse you know well. I was young and my blood was hot, and I lusted after both the drink and the tavern keeper's daughter." His voice, mellowed by the ale, was as rich and sweet as honey, a likely snare for a village girl.

He motioned to Meggy to fill his mug again. "By harvest I understood Bess was with child, but more important, I understood at last what my work was. I resolved to return to Oxford and begin. She threw a copper pot at my head as I left. I bear the scar still." Another swallow and another wipe on the sleeve.

"And what of the child?"

He shook his head. "It was my work that was important. It consumed me. I wanted to do the impossible, know the unknowable. And if I succeeded, I would defeat death itself. Naught was more important."

"But to leave without a thought. I wondered about you sometimes—what your name was, and what you looked like, and where—"

A shadow passed over his face. He took a deep breath and another swallow and set his mug down sharply. "Enough idle talk." He stood up. "I must return to the laboratorium."

"But, sir, can you not—"

"I have no time for petty matters," he said, turning for the stairs. "I have my work."

Petty matters? He thought she was but a petty matter? Meggy opened her mouth to protest. She imagined her gran's face frowning at her, and she put her fists down. I have done for the moment, she thought, but I will visit this again later. And wrapped in her cloak, she fell onto her pallet and into sleep.

Before first light the alchemist's voice echoed down the stairs and into her dreams. "Daughter," he was shouting, "come here to me. Make haste!"

Margret, Meggy said to herself, Margret, but she supposed *daughter* preferable to *mistress* or *err*. She stood and quickly tied her bodice and kirtle on over her smock.

He was at the furnace, pouring a powder into a vessel over the flames, when she entered. "Hasten, take the bellows. This fire must be kept exceedingly hot."

Meggy took the bellows and began a furious pumping. She began to sing: *O good lord judge and sweet lord judge, hold your hand awhile. Methinks I see my father come, riding many a mile.*

The alchemist stopped her with an abrupt motion. "Silence, you tweedling baggage! I must have silence. By my troth, in sooth you are worse than no help at all!"

Meggy's cheeks grew hot. The marble-hearted tyrant! Cold and ungenerous, he was unchanged from the man who had left her mother and forsaken his child before she was born.

A petty matter, he had called her. Did he think her a petty matter because she was lame? And what if she were whole? Her thoughts were all skimble-skamble as she pumped the bellows in silence. Although the fire stayed hot and the powder in the vessel turned to a silvery liquid, she came no closer to understanding that man in the shabby black gown who called her daughter.

At midday he said, "Enough," and Meggy gladly put the bellows down, for her arms ached from the pumping and her legs from standing. He took the vessel off the flame and put it on the table. "I must fully understand the ways of mercury," he muttered, "for it is said mercury carries the secret of transformation." He took a bottle from a shelf and poured a measure of clear liquid onto the mercury in the vessel. A thick red vapor formed and hovered over the surface, leaving bright red crystals in the bottom.

"Behold, mistress!" he shouted. "Red crystals! It is known that red is on silver's way to becoming gold." Her father's voice grew shrill with excitement. "If I could now remove the quality of redness from the crystals and add yellowness . . ." The arms of his gown flapped as he paced around the tiny room, nearly colliding with table here and shelf there. "Close, I am close, I am certain of it." He started for the stairs. "You there—err, mistress—wash these bottles. I must away. I must away." And he was gone.

Go to, Meggy thought, looking into the vessel. She saw no gold. Wat Tuttle in her village believed he could fly, but that did not make it so.

Meggy cleared the table and washed the bottles in the water bucket. She looked around. Her father was gone, and she was alone in a warm room. Here was her chance to wash the smoke from her hair, her smock, and her kirtle.

Her hair she let hang wet on her shoulders, and she spread her clothing on the furnace to dry. But the fire was yet too hot, and her kirtle scorched and sizzled. Ye toads and vipers, she thought as she gathered up her damp smock, ruined kirtle, and the water bucket and juggled them slowly down the stairs. She put on a clean smock and her other kirtle, her favorite, of Bristol red, and stuffed the ruined one into the bottom of her sack. She emptied the dirty water into the street and left the bucket by the door for the water carrier to fill. Then she sat and waited for her father to return. But when he did, he hurried past her up the stairs, saying nothing to her at all.

TWELVE

The heat was excessive for autumn, and the air heavy. The streets rang with the sounds of people making merry, but Meggy cared not. She sat at the table, mopey, alone, and plentifully hot.

Of a sudden the door banged open. "Come, Meggy Swann," Roger called. "We are off to the river in search of a breeze."

She looked up, hiding the joy she felt at seeing him, and said, "Pray, sir, pardon me. For a moment I mistook you for someone I did once know. Someone who swore he was a friend and then abandoned me to sink under my afflictions in this—"

"Nay, Meggy, be not spleeny. I was occupied with drilling the apprentices and learning a new part myself. Rein in your temper and join us, if the master can spare you."

"Spare me? Of late," Meggy said, "he labors all day and night and does not let me in nor make use of me." What did he now in his laboratorium? Why had he not again called for her?

"Well, then, let us be off," Roger said. "The queen will be barging to Westminster. If we make haste, we will see her!"

The queen! Her mopes and sulks forgotten, Meggy grabbed her walking sticks and followed Roger out the door.

The Grimms were gathered in the lane outside. "Well met, Mistress Meggy," said Mistress Grimm, straightening the girl's cap. "Well met, well met!" squealed the twins, while they danced and twirled in their impatience to be off.

Master Merryman sneered, and Master Grimm's face grew hard. "She will but delay us," he said, "limping and shuffling. Must we—"

Mistress Grimm pinched his arm, and he stepped aside to let Meggy pass.

Roger walked a few paces ahead of Meggy and stopped. He twirled and stopped and twirled again. Then he walked back toward her, his arms swinging like windmill blades.

"Why do you fidget so?" Meggy asked him. "You wiggle about like a water snake in the shallows. "

"Have you not noticed, Mistress Meggy, that I wear a splendid doublet and trunk hose?" He twirled around again and struck a pose so that the sun glinted off a gold earring in his ear. "You have not remarked upon me. Am I not fine? Do I not look a very picture?"

"You, my Lord Vanity, look the very picture of a fool, prancing and preening like that," said Meggy, and Violet Velvet snorted.

"Come, hurry, hurry," cried the twins, and each grabbed

one of Meggy's arms and began to run. The three fell aheap in the street.

"Fie upon it!" shouted Master Grimm. "Did I not say—"

"You, Ivory Silk," Mistress Grimm shouted as she slapped at the twins, "have a care for Mistress Meggy. And you, Silver Damask, are a thoughtless baggage!"

Roger helped Meggy up and handed her the fallen walking sticks. She was a bit bruised and dirty but oddly pleased that the twins had forgotten for a moment her lameness. "Pay him no mind," Roger said, gesturing toward Master Grimm striding on ahead. "He desired to see the hanging at Wapping in the Woze but was shouted down in favor of the river and the queen. As a consequence he is bad tempered as a man with a boil on his bum."

The twins had jumped to their feet and with hands all mucky from the street grabbed Roger's. "Come, Roger. Let us quick away!" And the three hurried around the corner onto Fish Street Hill.

Although Meggy went as quickly as she could, they stopped now and then for her to catch up. Master Grimm grimaced and grumbled. "Fie and fie again!" he said at last. "The queen is likely to be in France afore we reach the river with this laggard." Meggy stopped, her face burning. She would turn back, queen or no queen.

Master Merryman touched Master Grimm's arm and said, "You and the family hasten on, Cuthbert. Mistress Swann and I will follow at a more sedate pace."

Master Grimm grabbed Mistress Grimm with one arm and Violet Velvet with the other, and they hurried after Roger and the twins.

Meggy stood still, both grateful and fearful to find herself alone with the ill-favored Master Merryman, but he spoke softly and kindly. "Befitting the name of Grimm," he said, "Cuthbert has ever been churlish and spleeny. Pray pardon him."

"But," Meggy said, "he appears so merry."

"Ah, appears. You and I, Mistress Swann, know better than most how one can be misjudged because of how one appears." His good eye was heavy and sad, and his expression, she saw now, more woeful than sneering. "Will you walk with me, mistress?"

Meggy nodded. He walked slowly on, and drawing a great breath, she walked on beside him, stick-swing-drag. After a long moment she asked, "If Master Grimm be so much a scowling scold, why do you call him partner?"

"Grimm he may be," said Master Merryman, "but Cuthbert does run a fine company. Anywise, he will as long as he is allowed. Laws are becoming stricter and officials more vigilant. In time no player will be able to wear a wig or dance a jig less he is sponsored by some noble and licensed by the lord mayor. How we can accomplish that I know not." He shook his head.

"And playing pleases you?" she asked him.

"Aye, certes, it pleases me well. How else am I to hide this foul countenance of mine that shrivels flowers and sours milk? Still, I play but monsters and villains. No face paint could make me a hero."

Meggy's face grew warm with pity for Master Merryman and shame that she had not seen the man behind the scar. "You and I, Master Merryman," she said, "wear masks we cannot take off."

"Aye, Mistress Swann, well said." He gave a sneer that might have been a smile.

They approached the river, where half of London looked to be gathered. And where folk gather, so too do hucksters and cutpurses. Meggy took no interest in the cutpurses, as she had no purse to cut, but she inspected closely those peddlers selling ginger cakes, meat pies, baked apples. Sniffing deeply cost nothing.

Master Merryman bought a sack of sugared almonds, which he shared with Meggy and the Grimm children when they met once more. She sucked the sugar off each one slowly afore crushing the nut in her teeth and letting it all, the sweet and the crunchy, slide together down her rapturous throat.

The sound of music heralded the queen's approach. First came a barge holding a troupe of musicians playing loudly on lutes and flutes, sackbuts and viols and tambourines. Behind the barge, wherries darted to and fro, hired by folks who wished to get a closer look. Finally Meggy saw the queen's barge, painted red and yellow, adorned with flower garlands and gaily colored pennants. A dozen rowers in dazzling cream livery pulled in rhythm. Beneath a green silk canopy embroidered in gold, a lute player, strumming and singing, sat at the feet of a gilded chair. And on that chair was the queen. The queen! Such a day, Meggy thought, that offered sugared almonds and the queen! Her hair flamed red and gold, and her dress was ivory satin covered with pearls and emeralds. She looked, Meggy thought— how best might she state it?—she looked in sooth like a queen.

Church bells rang. Londoners called out, "God save your majesty!" and "Bless our Bess!" and, as Londoners often did, "A pox upon the cursed Spanish!" The queen smiled and waved.

"She saw us!" one of the twins shouted. "She knows us!" added the other. Roger took Violet Velvet by the hand, and they pushed their way through the crowd, hoping to make the queen look at them, too.

"Behold," shouted Ivory Silk, "the swans!" In the wake of the queen's barge, a flock floated silently by.

"Such graceful birds," said Mistress Grimm.

Gesturing toward the birds, Master Merryman said, "You are well named, Meggy Swann."

"Not so," said Meggy. "I have no grace. I wabble, I stumble, and I cannot dance."

"And these swans, their wings clipped to keep them near, cannot fly," said Master Merryman, "nor are they graceful on land, but they give us great pleasure nonetheless."

Meggy blushed as Roger, rejoining them, called out, "In sooth! 'Tis true!" and Mistress Grimm added, "Well said, Master Merryman, well said."

Master Grimm called his family to him. "Make haste," he said, "for I wish us safe home ere dark."

At the turning for Crooked Lane, Meggy bade farewell to Roger and the Grimms. To Master Merryman she said, "I hope you and Master Grimm may resolve your troubles soon. And I do humbly thank you for your kindness and the sugared almonds."

He winked at her with his good eye. "God save you, Mistress Swann," he said.

By the faint light of the moon, Meggy glimpsed several men wrapped in dark cloaks hurrying into the house at the Sign of the Sun. She followed quietly behind them and saw them start up the stairs. Meggy did not wish to follow farther, but curiosity and worry each took one of her hands and dragged her to the staircase. Fearing her sticks would make too much noise, she left them below and crept up the stairs on her hands and knees like a babe.

She sat on the topmost step and pushed the door open a crack. "All is in readiness," she heard someone say.

And the alchemist responded, "Then let him begin the doses now."

"To show our gratitude, Master Ambrose," said another someone.

Meggy heard the clink of coins and then her father saying, "Two gold sovereigns? But we agreed upon six."

"A mighty sum, which you shall have," the first someone said, "when I am required to announce the tragic death of

Sir Mortimer Blunt, our beloved Baron Eastmoreland." There was laughter and then footsteps moving toward the door.

It was past time for Meggy to haste away. In a panic she pushed herself down the stairs, sliding like a small boy on a snowy hill. It made her bum sting a bit but proved a useful way of escaping. By the time the men had bid their farewells and descended, the girl was curled up on her pallet, making soft snoring noises. She opened one eye and watched as the red-headed lout and his gorbellied companion stole out the door.

Her heart beat fast but silently, and her thoughts betumbled round and round. So she had not misunderstood. Master Peevish, Master Ambrose, her father, was indeed involved in something deadly. In murder. In payment he received the coins to pursue this Great Work of his. What was she to do? If she told no one, he would have his money and his work would proceed. But at what cost? He would be murderer, damned to Hell. Meggy also, belike, she thought with a shiver, for knowing but doing nothing. If she revealed what she had heard to someone who could stop him, her father might be seized. Burned at the stake or shorter by a head.

The specter of the Devil invaded her thoughts. She pulled her cloak over her head and wished for morning. Finally falling asleep, she dreamed that the queen had come to visit and Louise bit her and was sent to the gallows at Wapping in the Woze.

❧ THIRTEEN ❧

When Meggy climbed to the laboratorium the morning next, she had made a decision. Fearful and reluctant though she was, she would face the alchemist with what she had heard.

Master Ambrose was seated at the table, fingering two gold coins. He spun them and stacked them and spun them again. "As you see," he said, "I have of late come by a measure of gold, and there will be more anon. My Great Work shall continue."

"I heard the men who gave you the coins," Meggy said. "They wish you to dispatch someone." He did not deny it. "Are you not afeared? In sooth, would you see the world from atop a stick on London Bridge?"

Master Ambrose shrugged. "This gold enables my work and provides you with candles and a chicken pie now and again." He continued stacking and unstacking the coins. He said naught more but dropped them into the copper pot, where they fell with satisfying clinks.

"Even for your Great Work," Meggy asked, "will you really do murder?"

"You wrong me. I kill no one," said the alchemist. "I but supply a solution of white arsenic. What others do with it is their affair. Mayhap they want to kill rats or rabid dogs. Why, I hear there are places where women mix arsenic in face cream to whiten their complexions." He stood and pointed to a shelf. "Give me the tall flask."

She put it into his hands. "Why did they come to you?"

"For my expertise and my silence. They know my reputation."

He had a reputation as a poisoner, Meggy thought. He was her father and he murdered people. What did this mean about her?

"I need funds," he said, "if I am to continue my work. For a more powerful furnace so that I may experiment with other kinds of metals. For larger retorts and alembics." He swept his arm around the room, pointing with the flask. "For dishes, beakers, jars and vials, filters, strainers, and stirring rods. For mercury, sulfur, alum, vitriol, and borax. For copper and silver, pelicans and alembics and crucibles." He set the flask on the table. "If I could unlock the secret of transformation, if I could turn base metals into gold, I would not have to sell my soul. But until then, I do what I must do. And I am close, so close. This very morning from a calamine and copper solution I saw come forth a metal that is neither calamine nor copper but is changed in its very essence. I have transformed metal! It can be done."

His pale face shone, and Meggy thought she could see

a shadow of the passionate Oxford student. She shook her head. "No matter the value of your Great Work," Meggy said, "I do not believe it right to do murder for it."

"You need not murder anyone. You must just do as you are told until I have succeeded. Naught matters but my work. Naught."

"But I—"

He slammed his hand on the table. "Naught else matters, do you understand me, or have you not the wit?" He took some coins from the money pot. "Take these shillings and go to the bookshop at the sign of the White Hart at St. Paul's. Tell them you have come for *The Book of the Secrets of Alchemy*, composed by Galid, son of Jaziche. The bookseller will know the one. And return with haste. I must consult Galid at once."

Overnight the weather had turned cool and damp, chilling Meggy's bones and making her legs throb with pain. Her heart was as heavy as the dank air. She found the shop at the sign of the White Hart near the west gate of St. Paul's and bargained so sharply with the bookseller that she had sixpence left, which she would use to buy supper. Although Master Peevish never thought of his belly, hers argued with her fiercely if she did not eat somewhat regularly.

As she headed for home, the book in her sack, her thoughts became worries. What should she do? Her father believed his Great Work important enough to do murder. But was finding what he sought even possible? Would he risk his soul in pursuit of a foolish dream?

Meggy turned and headed down Paul's Chain and into the alley to Master Allyn's printing house. Master Allyn was attempting to work the great hand press with Gilly pulling at his leg and baby Robert asleep in one arm. "You find me somewhat discommoded," Master Allyn said. "Mistress Allyn is at the paper seller's haggling over the price, and I am nursery maid as well as printer."

"Belike you need help, Master Printer," Meggy said.

"Help wants pay," the printer responded.

Meggy sat on the stool and took Gilly onto her lap. The child put one hand in her mouth and twirled Meggy's hair with the other. Taking a deep breath, Meggy asked the question she had come to ask. "Master Allyn, what think you of the idea of transformation?"

"Transformation? Caterpillar to butterfly? Egg to chicken?" He grasped the lever on the press and pushed it forward.

"Transformation through alchemy," Meggy said. "Making gold. Finding the secrets of immortality and eternal youth."

"Wherefore," asked the printer, "do you ask these questions?"

"My father," she said. "Think you that he, with his alchemical learning, his minerals and metals, beakers and books, can find an elixir that will make all things perfect? He says he is close to success. What think you? Do you believe it possible?"

Master Allyn lifted the top of the press and pulled out a printed sheet. "In truth I know not," he said to Meggy, "but men with more learning than I have believe it." He held up the printed sheet. "I myself know only printing, changing speech to inky marks, capturing words and thoughts on paper for anyone to read. There are those who thought such a thing not possible, but here it is."

"Finding this elixir . . . what might a man rightly do to succeed at such a task? Could he break laws of God and man and be forgiven?"

The printer ceased what he was doing and looked at Meggy. "Mistress Swann, just what is it you are asking me?"

Meggy shook her head. "Naught, Master Printer. I was but wondering." She bade farewell to those at the printer's shop and made for Crooked Lane.

As she reached the end of Budge Row, Meggy heard faint music, lively and gay. She followed the sound to a large, brightly painted house whence came the sounds of horns and drums and a tinkling like water over the stones in Millford brook. Meggy leaned against the house and pulled herself as tall as she might in order to see in a window.

There was dancing inside. And what dancing! Not skipping round a maypole nor stamping in a Morris dance. As the music swirled around them, ladies dressed in the colors of the sunrise leapt and fluttered as they were twirled and tossed by gentlemen in bright doublets and silk hose. Meggy pressed her face against the window. If I had sound legs, she thought, I would dress in such colors and wear silk hose and dance everywhere instead of walking, I would.

"Pardon, sir," she said to a gentleman in padded yellow doublet and grass green shoes who approached the house. "What is this place?"

"Ahh, Mistress Crookleg, naught to interest you here," he said. "It is a dancing house where people who are sound of body come to learn the fashionable dances." He pulled a silken handkerchief from his sleeve and waved it. "Take your tottery self away."

Another young man joined him and, with a twirl and a jump, cried, "Let us haste, Robert, to the frisks and flyings, galliards and galops!"

The young men slapped each other's backs and, laughing, entered the dancing house.

Fie on them, Meggy thought as she wabbled toward Crooked Lane once more. Fie on them, with their strong legs that could leap and dance. Fie on them who had no care for those who could not, those who would need magic to—ye toads and vipers! Suppose her father indeed found the elixir he sought, and it could transform her. Make her legs straight so she could walk without wabbling and without pain. So she could dance! Would that not be wondrous?

Meggy shook her head. Roger and Master Allyn thought her father's work possible, and the cooper had spoken of magic and marvels. She wished to believe it, but she had yet seen no sign of transformation or perfection or gold. She could imagine bears and angels and cream cakes in the clouds, but that did not make them real. Likely her father was just Sir Boastful, all cock-a-hoop about naught. And in sooth she could not think it worth doing murder for.

"Sir, here is the volume you require," Meggy said as she entered the laboratorium. The air was heavy, thick with smoke, and as hot as she imagined Hell might be.

He said nothing but continued stirring a silver-colored mixture in a crucible. "Work the bellows, girl," he said. "This must be kept hot." After a time he strained the mixture from the crucible, rinsed it in water, and took the particles that washed out and put them back into the crucible.

"Give me the *aqua fortis*," he said, pointing to a large bottle, and Meggy did. He poured the liquid into the crucible. An acrid vapor arose. He poured off the liquid, and she saw that fewer of the particles remained. Again and again he poured the *aqua fortis* into the crucible and poured it off again. Again and again he rinsed and strained the mixture. Fewer and fewer of the particles remained, but they shone brighter and brighter.

Meggy's heart thumped. Was that gold she saw forming in the bottom of the crucible? Was it growing from base metal into gold? Had her father done it?

"Sir," she began, but he hushed her with a wave.

"No prattle," he said. She continued pumping in silence.

Darkness fell, and still they labored in the hot, smoky laboratorium. Meggy did not heed the aching of her legs or the complaining of her belly as she worked.

"Enough," Master Ambrose said at last. Meggy put down

the bellows, picked up a candle, and peered into the crucible. What she saw near took her breath away. There in the bottom was a tiny coil of what even the wary Meggy might call gold.

"Is it gold?" Meggy asked the alchemist in a whisper. "Truly gold?"

He nodded.

"Then you have done it! You have made gold." It was a tiny amount, to be sure, but he had transformed common metal into gold. There it was in the crucible. Now he could make all the gold he needed. He would no longer need to plot murder but could continue his Great Work until he succeeded in finding the elixir of life.

Mayhap he would let her use it, just as she had imagined. She was overcome with wondering. Would he? Would it be powder, liquid, solid, vapor? Would it smell sweet or sting her nose as she breathed? How would it heal her legs? Would she rub it on? Drink it? Just touch it? Would it work instantly or take a few moments? Would there be a flash of lightning or puff of smoke?

And then Crooked Meggy would walk and run and, aye, dance. She would be transformed into someone straight and strong. And her father would come to value her. For this, she decided, she would labor hard and uncomplaining at his side. And then someday Crooked Meggy would dance. She would have grass green shoes and she would dance. Hope crept into the house and settled in Meggy's heart.

"Daughter," Master Ambrose said, interrupting her imaginings. "Daughter, pay heed. I am calling you. Hand to me that—"

"But sir, are you not gobsmacked? You have made gold! Just as you said you would."

The man slammed his hand down on the table so hard it trembled. "Foolish girl! As if the making of gold were that simple. A trick, that is all it is."

A trick? Meggy found it hard to breathe.

"A trick," he repeated, "separating flecks of gold from ore that contains both gold and silver. I can also rub a silver object with a gold-ash-soaked rag until it gleams gold. I can grind gold and lead to a fine powder and coat a copper object until it shines gold. Or melt copper and silver with gold to make a great amount of what appears to be gold. But I produce only imitations of gold, not true transformation. I do tricks to fool the gullible into believing and parting with large sums of money in hopes of receiving large amounts of gold." He sat down at the table and put his head in his hands. "In sooth I can no more make gold than your blasted goose can."

As much as Meggy had not wanted to believe, she now did not want to doubt. "But you said you were so close," she began, "and I see gold . . ."

The alchemist looked up. "It can be done, I am certain it can be done, but I need more equipment, more material, a larger laboratory, a proper assistant. And for that I need money. A great deal of money." He picked up the cooled coil of gold and rubbed it between his fingers. "This should convince the fools to invest in my work, but I shall need to separate more. Mistress . . . err, fetch the—"

But Meggy was on her way down the stairs, thumping hard on each step. The prating mountebank! He had gulled her into believing for a moment, but he was a fraud! Let him perform his tricks. Let him even do his murder. Let him be taken and his head be mounted on the bridge for all to see. She cared not.

A proper assistant? And what of Mistress . . . Err?

Meggy dropped carelessly onto her pallet and wept. She was sorry she had seen the dancing house and the coil of gold, that she had allowed herself to hope her father's Great Work might mean her transformation. He was but a fraud and a murderer, and she would likely never dance in grass green shoes.

She dreamed that night of the heads on London Bridge. One wore a crown. 'Twas the baron, she knew. His head was impaled on a stick. Her walking stick! She woke with a start and a cry. She knew full well what the dream was saying. If the baron died, it was her doing.

If she had not heard the men in the laboratorium, she would know nothing of their plans. If she knew nothing, it would not be upon her to do anything. But she had heard, and it was now in her hands.

Morning came at last. Yesterday's rain had blown away, and the day dawned warm, lit by an autumn sun that turned the mist to gold. There was true alchemy, Meggy thought as she headed for a cookshop on Thames Street. Not the tricks in her father's laboratorium.

Her thoughts all betumbled, Meggy missed her turning and found herself at the river. The air rang with the cries of seagulls fighting over scraps and the calls of the peacocks in the gardens of the rich. The breeze blew her cloak about and ruffled the hair of the heads mounted on the bridge.

She gazed up at them. What should she do? Should she trouble herself to stop the baron's murder? And save her father, fraud that he be?

Who could offer counsel? Roger, she thought finally. I will have speech with Roger.

❧ F O U R T E E N ❧

Meggy turned and walked once again up Fish Street Hill and over to Pudding Lane. Belike it was because she had no goose to battle, she thought, but the walk seemed right easy this time.

"Good morrow, lass," said Mistress Grimm as she opened the door to the girl. "Come join us for a comfit and a bit of gossip." She led Meggy into the kitchen, handed her a sweet, and pulled another stool up to the table.

Meggy looked about but did not see Louise. "How does my goose?"

"She bit Master Grimm, she did," said Mistress Grimm, "which was much the worst thing she could do."

"Worse than the time she chewed Master Merryman's new leather glove," said Ivory Silk. Or was it Silver Damask?

"Worse than the time she left fresh droppings in Roger's shoe," said Silver Damask. Or was it Ivory Silk?

"Even worse than the time she ate half a blackberry pie and puked it up again," said Violet Velvet.

114

"So Louise has gone to live with my uncle Fletcher near Westminster," said Mistress Grimm.

"He does not think to eat her?" Meggy asked.

"Nay, sweeting, do not fret. He be grateful for her bad-tempered hissing and honking. Keeps the mice and rats away, he says. And she and his duck are become great friends."

Meggy grieved for a moment. Louise had been *her* friend, for a long while her only friend. But certes, geese are not known for their loyalty.

"We were talking of the queen," said Mistress Grimm as she picked up an apple to peel and slice. "Of her marriage to the Duke of Alençon."

"Never will she marry him," said Violet Velvet, who, like the other girls, was sewing on some brightly colored stuff.

"Because he is a Frenchman?" Meggy asked, for that was all she knew of him.

Violet shook her head.

"Because he is too young?" asked Ivory Silk. Or Silver Damask?

"Nay," said Violet. "He is old enow."

"Because he is a Catholic?" asked Silver Damask. Or Ivory Silk.

"Nay again," said Violet. "The queen will never marry him because his nose be too big. And marked from the pox. I do not think the queen would like to look at his big, pockmarked nose every day."

"Especially at breakfast," said one twin.

"Especially if she were eating a sausage," said the other.

Amid the laughter, the twins began to poke each other with their needles. "Cease your brabbling," Meggy said, "and I will show you something I learned of my granny." She took a long strip of apple peel from Mistress Grimm and gave it to Ivory Silk (or was it Silver Damask?). "Throw this peel over your right shoulder, and it will reveal the first letter of the name of your true love." The girl did. "Now," said Meggy, "what letter did it form?"

The twins leapt from their chairs and knelt down, peering at the curled peel. "It is an *S*," said one twin.

"Nay, it be an *F*," said the other. "*F* for Francis! Francis Shore, the fencing master, is your true love!"

"Ne'er! Fie upon him! You do it, Meggy," said the other twin. So Meggy threw a bit of peel over her shoulder.

"*O*?" one girl asked, looking closely..

"*P*?" asked the other.

And then both together they shouted, "*R!* 'Tis an *R*, for Roger!"

Meggy, blushing, said, "Nay, nay, the peel is but reminding me why I have come. Is Roger about? 'Tis most important that I speak with him."

Mistress Grimm picked up another apple and began to pare it. "The gentlemen are performing this day at the Cross Keys Inn on Gracechurch Street. Know you the one, past the Church of St. Denis?"

Meggy did not, but nodded, for she thought she could find it, and she did, beyond the church, as Mistress Grimm had said. The courtyard was packed not with coaches and carts, as one might expect, but with people crowded around a scaffold at the front.

"Good day, young mistress. Pay yer penny here to see the play," said a snaggletoothed woman at the entry.

"I be no playgoer," Meggy told her. "I would talk with Roger Old—"

"Ye must pay yer penny. Everyone pays."

"I have no penny, but 'tis important that I see Roger. I swear not to peek at the play."

The woman looked at Meggy's walking sticks. "Ah, the show be nearly over. Go you in."

Meggy thanked the woman and made her way into the courtyard, where she was assaulted by the smell of onions and stale ale. All around her, people shoved and shouldered, shouted and laughed, and pelted the platform with roasted nuts and apples.

Despite her promise to the ticket woman, Meggy hoped to see a wee bit of this occasion called a play. "Make way," she said, "make way," as she tried to push to the front with her walking sticks. People looked down at her, clutched the purses at their waists, and turned back to the play. The girl finally nudged her way close enough to the platform to see and hear.

Up on the platform two men in embroidered doublets leapt about, with shouts and a furious waving of swords, until a beauteous lady fell in a swoon at their feet. The taller man took the lady in his arms. The other man ran him through with his sword like a capon on a skewer, and blood streamed onto the stage. There was a good bit of weeping and moaning, both in the play and in the audience.

Meggy's heart stopped for a moment. She cried out, "The poor man. Is he truly dead?"

The fellow next her said with a kind smile, "It be but chicken blood, mistress, drawn by wooden swords."

Chicken blood? Swords made of wood? It had been so real. This then was what Roger meant by playing. These people were pretending wondrous things and making them seem true.

Meggy forgot the crowds and the courtyard, the chicken blood and wooden swords. She was swept up and far away.

A king's army battled a monster, a queen died, a king died, there was more blood, and everyone was aggrieved. Then the players came out and bowed—even the dead ones—and danced a little jig, were pelted with more roasted nuts, and climbed down off the platform.

The play was done. Meggy was once more in a reeky courtyard, slipping on apple cores. Her cheeks were wet with tears and her heart beat like a bird in her chest. She felt such pity, such anger, such joy, and such disappointment that she could scarce contain it all. A play was a marvelous thing, she thought, to inspire such a tumult of feeling.

As the crowds pushed out, Meggy held on to a corner of the platform lest she be swept into the tide of playgoers like herring in fishing season. She heard a man's voice from behind the scaffold. "Good Master Player," she called, "I am in search of Roger Oldmea—ham. Roger Oldham. I saw him not in the play. Know you where might I find him?"

A gold-crowned head peeked around the platform. Master Grimm. Go to! That was why the king, even in all his finery, had looked like a sack of flour on legs. "Ah, Mistress Swann, come to see us. How liked you the play?" he asked.

"'Twas wondrous grand," she said. "I never knew of such a thing. I would be a player, too, if only women could be players. But it was excellent to watch."

"Come sit with me and tell me more. Tell me how I outbraved and outbragged the other players." he said. "'Pon my honor, I did play brilliantly. Never was a king more kingly and a death more deadly. Come, tell me."

"Nay, I must find Roger."

"Go then, ill-mannered girl. I shall find some other one to dazzle. Roger be yon, behind the stage, leaving off his costume."

She went where he pointed, and there was the beauteous lady who had swooned so distressingly. "Good mistress," Meggy began, and the lady turned. It was Roger. Roger! Meggy thought she would recognize that nose anywhere, even under a shipload of paint.

"By my troth, it be the fetching Mistress Swann, come to see me play," said Roger. "Was I not grand? Do I not have the most magnificent gown?" He twirled. "And see my—"

Were all players this boastful? Meggy wondered. "Enough, Sir Pridesome," she said to him. "I am confounded and bestraught and do seek your counsel."

He curtsied, in tolerable style for one with such shoulders. "At your service, Dame Impatient. Let me become Roger again. I shall beg off from my fellows and escort you home, and you will tell me what you want of me."

Roger returned in a moment, the golden curls and lace ruffles gone, wearing a leather jerkin over his doublet and hose.

"More wages gone for clothes, Oldmeat?" Meggy asked.

"Is it not fine? Real Spanish leather. Master Grimm grew too stout for it and now it is mine. Do I not look lordly?" He twirled.

"You grow vain, Oldmeat," she said.

"Not at all. I have always been vain. It be my tragic flaw. In all the very best dramas the hero has a tragic flaw." He started to walk across the courtyard, and Meggy wabbled alongside him.

"Enough of your prattling, my Lord Vanity," Meggy said. "Tragic reminds me wherefore I am here. I fear my father is involved in misdeeds that might leave someone tragically dead and me tragically alone. I pray your help, Oldmeat."

Roger stopped. "I do believe that the first rule of asking a favor of someone is to call that someone not Oldmeat but instead Roger."

There was silence for a moment, but at last she said, "Aye, *Roger*. Now hearken, *Roger*, and be still. Men came to my father, *Roger*. They would poison a noble lord called Baron Eastmoreland, and they sought my father's assistance."

"Poison? Nay, 'tis not so. What has the master to do with poisons?" He scratched his head, and his earring winked in the sunshine. "But I did hear comings and goings of strange

120

men in the night . . . and he did send me on useless errands at times . . ."

"'Tis true. My father supplies poison for the elimination of rats and mice and unloved lords. And he is a fraud, doing tricks to cheat people out of their money. He be a poor father, indeed. But in truth a poor father is better than no father at all. I do not wish to see his head on London Bridge. Oh, Oldme— Roger, will you help me choose the right course?"

Roger took her arm. "Come, we will visit a cookshop and eat pigs' trotters by the river while you tell me more."

~❦ FIFTEEN ❦~

Meggy and Roger took their food to the ruins of a wharf by the river. They sat on stones warm from the afternoon sun. The music of lutes and viols could be heard from the windows of a big house nearby, and barges with silken canopies sailed past, followed by a silent procession of swans like lanterns floating on the river.

Meggy told Roger what she had overheard. "I could accuse him to the watch," she concluded, "but then he would be seized. Or worse."

Roger stopped chewing to ask, "And if you do nothing?"

Meggy sighed. "Indeed, I would prefer to do nothing, for it would mean less trouble for me. But a man would lie dead, my father would be murderer, and I would know it. And God would know it. I would be known to all as the daughter of a murderer." Tears filled Meggy's eyes, slipped down her cheeks, and splashed on her bodice.

Finally she snuffled and wiped her face with her kirtle. "I cannot do nothing. I must try to save the baron and keep my father's head on his shoulders." She sighed again. She and Roger sat in silence for a time, and then Meggy asked, "Why does someone seek to dispatch this Baron Eastmoreland?"

"He is an honest man, it is said, loyal to the queen, and thus misliked by those who are not."

"Including," Meggy said, "his gorbellied food taster and an odious ginger-haired man." She thought a moment, chewing on her lip, and then said, "Mayhap if we warned the baron that there was danger, that he should be wary and look to his food, he would be on his guard."

"And how might you do that? Mark me well, Meggy. He is a baron, and you be the daughter of an alchemist from Crooked Lane. Think you to knock at his door and say, 'Open to me. I would have speech with the baron'?"

"Who might have speech with him then? A water carrier? Fishmonger? Chimney sweep?"

"Meggy Swann," said Roger, "you know a poor pennyworth about barons. Tradesmen speak not with barons but with their servants."

"A letter then. What think you of a letter?"

"Know you how to write a letter?"

"You do."

Roger nodded. "Aye, in Latin. Does he read Latin?"

Meggy shrugged.

"Have you paper? Ink? A pen?"

She shook her head.

"We know not where he lives. We could not get past his door. And he would pay us no heed anywise."

"Roger, all you say is not, not, not," Meggy said, slapping her hand against the stones. "I pray you be more help than that."

"What then be your will, my lady?" Roger asked. "Shall I fly in through his window with a warning in my mouth? I say do not fret over this matter. It concerns your father and the baron. 'Tis naught of your affair."

Meggy banged one of her sticks against the ground. "Old-meat, you are a craven coward and no use to me at all!"

Roger stood and bowed with a sweep of his cap. "Then I shall leave you, Mistress Crosspatch," he said, and turned and walked away.

"Go then, you writhled, beetle-brained knave!" she shouted. "You churl, you slug, you stony-hearted villain! May onions grow in your ears!"

Meggy stood and slowly wabbled toward home. Where Fish Street Hill crossed Crooked Lane, she saw her father, head down into the wind, hurrying to the house. He looked so worn and so worried that she was filled with pity despite herself. Aye, he was cold, remote, willful, hard, and selfish, a fraud and a trickster, mayhap even villainous and a black-hearted murderer. He had left her mother with child and his daughter before he knew her, had sent for her but did not want her, and now sometimes made her feel like a ha'penny, small and not worth very much. But such as he was, he was her father. She would not let him be but a head on London Bridge. She would warn the baron and then do what she could to help her father with his Great Work. And chicken-hearted Roger must be made to help.

Meggy did not turn for home but climbed to Pudding Lane, cursing the boy for causing her to chase after him. Finally, stepping carefully over pigs' innards steaming in the sunshine, she arrived at the Grimms'.

Master Grimm and Master Merryman were leaving the house as Meggy arrived. Master Grimm grumbled, "No time. We have no time for you," and strode off. But Master Merryman smiled sadly and spoke. "We are to see about the purchase of a wagon. Without patronage it be right hard to secure a space to perform. We may have to return to the road." He shook his head. "Even there belike we will not be safe from the law."

Roger, he told Meggy, had gone with friends to the Bellowing Bull on Candlewick Street. Meggy hastened there. A pox on Roger, she thought. If he was cupshot, up to his eyes in ale, he would be no use to her.

The windows of the inn were thrown open to the day's warmth, and Meggy peered in each one until she found Roger.

The other young men at his table were carousing, teasing and laughing, but a downcast Roger sat quietly. "Roger," Meggy called softly, but not softly enough. The entire tableful of fellows turned to her.

"What ho!" shouted one. "A maiden with the sweetest face this side of sugared plums beckons us."

Roger looked up. "Begone, Meggy," he said.

"No, I pray you, Roger, come hither. I want you."

"Oh fortunate Roger," one of the boys at the table called. And another, "Would that your sweetheart wanted me!"

Sweetheart? Ne'er! Impossible! She had no desire for a sweetheart. But belike if she had . . .

Roger was blushing red as a summer sunset as he hurried to her side. "What?" he asked.

"Roger, be you codswalloped?"

"Nay, I am as sober as a newborn babe, not that it be your affair."

Meggy nodded. "Good," she said, and she began as she had practiced on the way. "I have resolved to see the baron, myself, without you, as you will not. It must be done. I care not for the danger, although if I am assaulted or imprisoned, 'twill be on your head for compelling me to go alone. And so farewell, Roger, if it should happen that we ne'er see each other again."

"How will you find him, Lady Obstinate?"

"I will ask. And ask. And ask. I will ask every living soul in London until I find someone who knows where lives this cursed baron. Now, I say again, fare thee well."

Roger sighed a sigh that could have blown the entire English fleet to France. "The baron dwells off Dowgate, near the river."

"How know you that?"

"I asked," he said. "And I will attend you, as you have known all this time I would."

Meggy smiled as they turned for Dowgate Street. 'Twas true. She had known.

Meggy and Roger walked a middling long way down from Candlewick Street and over on Thames Street. On one side of Dowgate Street were shops, taverns, and houses much the same as in the rest of London. On the other side was a residence that was nearly a city unto itself. Beyond a short wall of stone, Meggy saw, was a jumble of large redbrick buildings—towers, chapel, stables, and various chambers—set in a garden with abundant trees and a stretch of grass down to the river.

They stopped before the vast gatehouse. Meggy cleared her throat and called out to a face in a window, "Good morrow, good sir. Be you the baron?"

Roger poked her. "Clotpole! He is but the gatekeeper."

The face attached itself to a gross-bellied man who came through the door and stood before them, legs apart. "Be off with ye! No beggars here."

Meggy frowned, remembering the similar welcome given her by her father. She pulled herself as tall as she could. "We are not beggars. We would have speech with the baron."

The man laughed and rubbed his nose. "She would have speech with the baron! I would be knighted by the queen! Now off, I say!"

"But we bear a message for—"

He thrust his great belly toward them. "Do ye wish me to call the dogs?" Roger took Meggy's arm and pulled her away.

Men came and went through the gatehouse, but Meggy

could see no way of attaching herself to them and sneaking past the gateman. Dowgate was crowded with peddlers and hawkers and vendors, but they were all shooed away from the baron's gate. All but the ballad seller, for the gateman and passersby both stopped and listened as he sang, offering the last words, confession, and dying declaration of one Anne Fogget, hanged that very morning for the crime of murdering her husband: *My husband coming home somewhat in drink, as he was going to bed,* the ballad seller sang, *I took an axe I had prepared, and clove him in the head.* Meggy shivered, imagining the last words and dying confession of an alchemist of the city, hanged for preparing poison for a noble lord.

She pulled Roger away from the gate. He bought herring pies from a passing peddler, and they walked to the river to eat. Pigeons and sparrows and gulls cried as they fought over scraps of fish and other bits from the gutters. Roger took a large bite of his pie and wiped his mouth on his sleeve. "We have tried, Meggy," he said, "but we cannot—"

"Cannot, will not, would not!" Meggy said. "Do you wish to see my father's head spinning in the wind on London Bridge? Hear his last confession sung on London street corners? We must think of something."

"You are as stubborn as a donkey with sore feet! What think you to try next? Tying a message on one of those pigeons and letting him fly to the baron? Or mayhap you will take flight over the baron's walls and sing a song at his window." Roger began to sing in a surprisingly sweet voice.

Oh Baron, most loyal,
Although you recoil,
I must tell you this:
Something is amiss.
You must not partake
Of comfits or cake
For—

He began to laugh so hard at his own foolishness that he slipped and dropped his pie into the water, whereupon it was fought over by ducks until it sank to the bottom of the Thames.

"Belike you deserved that, Master Ninny," said Meggy, handing him the remains of her own pie.

"We can do no more." He reached a hand to her. "Let us leave this—"

"Ye toads and vipers, Oldmeat!" Meggy hissed. "Now my father will do murder, and he will be seized, and the baron will be dead, and I will be alone. I want—"

"You want! You want! Mistress Margret Swann, you are the most selfish, ungrateful wench I ever did know." Roger shook his head, and the feather in his cap wobbled sadly. "You think only of yourself and your own concerns. I would I ne'er had met you and wish ne'er to meet you again." He hastened away, leaving Meggy there.

She sat and watched the birds. "Fie on him, the mewling moldwarp," she said, but the birds said nothing.

Finally Meggy made her way back to the baron's. She approached the gatehouse once more.

"Be it you again?" the gatekeeper asked. He sneezed and wiped his nose on his sleeve. "Get you gone."

"Master Gatekeeper," Meggy said, "I know you will not allow that I see the baron, but if it please you, will you take a message to him? 'Pon my honor, he is in grave danger, for—"

The gatekeeper stepped toward Meggy and waved his hands at her. "Go, I said! Clear the way. The baron has no interest in the fancies of a crippled ragamuffin. Go!"

"But—"

"But no! Go away." He sneezed and turned his back to her.

Ye toads and vipers, thought Meggy, but this saving of someone's life takes a goodly amount of effort.

She turned and walked back toward Crooked Lane. Fish Street Hill was teeming with folk. Peddlers, costermongers, and chimney sweeps milled about, crying their wares to passing merchants, sailors, and fine folk in cart-wheel ruffs and feathered hats.

A ballad seller climbed on an overturned crate and called, "Gentlemen, ladies, pay heed. Hear of treason in our city." Treason? Meggy stopped, fearing to hear her father's name. "Hear a new ballad," he continued, "recounting the dangerous shooting of a gun at court." A gun? And he began:

> *Weep, weep, still I weep,*
> *And shall do till I die*

To think upon the gun that shot
At court so dangerously.

As the ballad seller described the events of July, when a stray bullet had narrowly missed the queen in her barge on the river, those gathered to listen muttered and grumbled. "Hang 'im!" shouted a man in a blue padded doublet. "God save the queen!" added others.

And then Meggy had an idea. People stopped to listen to ballad sellers and paid heed to their words. So she would write a ballad about the baron and the ginger-haired lout and sing it outside the baron's house. Someone would hear and warn the baron. The lout would be imprisoned and her father free. It was an inspired idea, Meggy thought, and she did not need Roger anywise.

✎ SIXTEEN ✎

Her father did not return at all that night, which Meggy knew, for she lay long awake, planning her ballad. "The Ballad of a Red-Headed, Black-Hearted, Pig-Eyed Lout," she would call it. She must be sly, use stealth and hugger-mugger, and not just blurt out the plot. It must be a real ballad with poetry and rhyme, but yet a clear enough warning so that when the right person heard, he would understand. And she must not reveal her father's hand in the plot. Could she do all that?

She lay on her pallet, rhyming and unrhyming, trying this word and that. "You lack-witted oaf," she said to herself, flopping over and back again, "a sausage could be a better poet than you." And, "No, no, no one will understand and I will be shamed." Her face grew moist, not so much from the labor of composing the ballad as from the mighty swings she took from despair to hope and back again. Finally, long after midnight, she repeated her song to herself once more. It would serve. But how to make certain it reached the ears of the right person? She pondered for a moment, and then—of course, she would have it printed! Aye, she would have it printed and sell it to every man going through the baron's gate. Certes someone would make sure it got to the man himself.

Should she tell her father what she was about? Or was it better if he did not know until after she had succeeded? What would he think? Would he be grateful or accuse her once again of meddling? She had no answers, so she pulled her cloak over her and nestled into the pallet. She dreamed of herring and dead birds and Louise's head on London Bridge.

In the morning she went again to Master Allyn. "I be here to make a bargain with you," she told him. "I have writ a ballad I would have printed. I will pay for it by selling other ballads and broadsides for you." She motioned to a printed stack on the table. "If those do sit unsold any longer, they will be old and stale and good for naught but plugging the holes in your shoes. Let me sell them."

The printer thought a moment and then said, "It seems a fair bargain. So you are a poet?"

She hesitated. Should she tell him the truth? Fearing he might be reluctant to be involved in her scheme, she said only, "Aye, sometimes I am a poet."

"Well, little poet, give me your ballad and I will set it in type."

"I know what I wish to say, I know my letters and read some, but I have no writing."

"Sing it to me then, and I shall write it." She did, using a tune that her granny had taught her.

"'Tis a most interesting ballad," he said when they had finished. "How did you come by it?"

Meggy answered, "I have a fine imagination," which was true. But she added nothing about the plot she had overheard or her father's part in it.

The printer began to pull metal letters from a box and arrange them into words on a composing stick. Though the letters were backwards, he pulled them with a speed that astonished Meggy. Then he moved the letters a line at a time onto a rack. He finished the sheet with the legend he used on all his broadsides, "Imprinted at the shop of John Allyn off Paul's Chain, near Ludgate," then wiped his hands on his apron.

This matter was taking a goodly long time, so Meggy said, "Mayhap I can assist you in some way." Taking one of the leather balls, the printer showed her how to smear ink on it and then rub it against the letters until they, too, were inked.

The man watched her carefully. "From all your years with the walking sticks," he said, "your hands and arms be right strong and nimble." She looked down at her hands, surprised. She had never thought they might have value, just that her legs did not.

He put the rack of inky letters onto the press and laid a piece of paper over it, grasped the lever, and pressed forward, so that the top of the press sank down against the paper. "How many copies are you wishing?" he asked Meggy.

She frowned, not knowing. One would be sufficient, were it to get to the right body. But to be safe, she said, "Twenty?"

"As you will, mistress." The printer pulled a printed sheet from the press and laid it on the table to dry. This he did until he had a stack of twenty. He handed one to Meggy.

She held the broadside in her two hands with a tingle of pride and delight. She had done this—she had bethought it, she had written it, she had helped to print it. And then a quiver of fear stirred her. What had she done and what would it bring her?

With a shake of her head and a sharp inhale, Meggy took the broadsides with her ballad and a great many others to sell for a ha'penny each, and she put them in her sack. She slipped her arms through the handles and the sack hung down her back. Slowly she wabbled to the door. "Mistress Meggy, I fear this is too much for you," the printer said. He put his hand on her arm.

"Leave off, Master Printer. I will do this." She stopped, and added, "I thank you, Master Printer, for your service and your trust."

Down Watling Street to Budge Row and thence to Candlewick she went. Master Allyn was right—the heavy sack made her going difficult, and a cold wind was rising, but her mind was set upon this deed, and her stubbornness was as persistent as her pain. She turned south toward the river and Dowgate.

Before the baron's great residence, she put down her sticks and leaned against the wall. Pulling broadsides and ballads from her sack, she called, "Come and buy. Come and buy," as she had heard the ballad sellers calling. "Come and buy"— she looked at the broadsides in her hand—"'The Ballad of

Lady Margery and the Cook.' Or perhaps 'The True and Last Confession of Richard Dowling, Murderer and Thief.' 'Tis a sorrowful lamentation with woodcut illustrations, sung to the tune of 'All in a Garden Green.'"

People came and went past the baron's gate. Some avoided her, casting suspicious or pitying glances at her walking sticks, but some stopped to listen, and others even paid a ha'penny for a copy of a ballad. Whenever a man or men came or went through the gate, she sang her own ballad.

> *I am a man of high renown*
> *Attendant to a lord.*
> *I am a man of villainous heart*
> *And poison is my sword.*

No one paid heed.

She moved closer to the gate. The lardy gatekeeper peered out his window at her but did not chase her away. She sang of a murder in Wiltshire and a sea serpent off Dungeness and of Robin Hood rescuing Will Stutly from the sheriff. She sold not a few copies and dropped the coins into the sack. Emboldened by her success, she sang louder, and people stopped to listen. So she tried her own ballad again.

> *My flaming hair, my piggish eyes*
> *Mark me as a fiend.*
> *And I will dispatch my goodly lord,*
> *Although he serves the queen.*

He is a traitor, listen well,
I tell you verily.
He plots against his honest lord
And there will murder be.

Her voice grew tired, her hair tangled in the wind, and her legs ached. Many times she thought to leave and find her pallet, but she sang on. Finally as midday turned to late afternoon, several gentlemen passed, talking and laughing, making for the baron's gate. Meggy stopped singing. The ginger-haired man was among them. Were they all in the plot? Would they hear and understand and throw her into the river with the fishes? Or might one of them be the baron's true friend and warn him?

She took a chance and a deep breath and sang.

So eat, my lord, and drink the wine,
You will not fall down sick
Until the fatal time has come
For the dose of the arsenic.

He is a traitor, listen well,
I tell you verily
He plots against his honest lord
And there will murder be.

So barons all, both west and east,
I cannot tell you more.

But there is a traitor in this land
As I have said afore.

Yes, barons all, both west and east,
I cannot tell you more.
But there is a traitor in this land . . .

One of the men making their way in turned to her. "Where found you that, girl?" he asked Meggy quietly. "Who gave you that?"

A lump the size of Master Grimm sat in her throat. "'Tis the newest ballad. Everyone be singing it. Will you buy?" she asked, and then swallowed a mighty swallow.

The man gave her a ha'penny, took a copy of the ballad, and stood by the gatehouse to read. His brow furrowed as he looked at the ballad sheet and then at the men passing into the baron's yard. With determined step he followed them.

Meggy let her breath out with a great whoosh. She took her sticks and her sack and wabbled slowly back to Master Allyn's printing house. She could not be certain the baron was warned, but she had done all she could. And without Roger.

Master Allyn took the money she brought him and counted out eight ha'pennies, which he gave back to Meggy for her very own.

Fourpence! Enough for a chicken pie. And apples and a wedge of cheese. Or a fruit tart with cream. Heading home with visions of a table laden with food, she passed a glove maker's stall. Hungry as she was, her hands pained her worse than her belly. Fourpence would not buy fine leather gloves, but belike she could find a pair of thick woolen mittens to protect her hands.

In a neighboring stall Meggy saw a small toy horse, carved of a fine dark wood with a tail of creamy wool. She left the gloves and the fruit tart and bought instead salve for her sore hands, half a loaf of fresh bread, and the horse.

The sky was growing darker as she turned onto Crooked Lane. She entered the cooper's shop and greeted the cooper. "Might I have speech with Master Nicholas?" she asked.

The boy came down from the room above. He smiled a watery smile when he saw Meggy and asked, "Have you come with another story for me?"

"Nay, not today, but see who has climbed into my sack and now nickers furiously to escape," she said as she pulled out the horse.

"Go to!" Nicholas said. "'Tis most fine. Be it yours?"

"Nay," said Meggy, "'tis yours." She felt her gran smile on her and heard her say, You gladden me, wee Meggy, and make me proud. Meggy's heart warmed.

She let herself into the house at the Sign of the Sun. Belike she should tell her father what she had done. No light showed from the laboratorium nor from his chamber. Had he not yet come home? Or was he already abed? Her travels of the day had left her weary and sore, so she lay down on her pallet, stomach full of bread and heart full of Nicholas's joy. And she had no dreams at all.

❧ SEVENTEEN ❧

The day brought rain. Meggy watched drops dance down the window. She had delayed having speech with her father but could delay no longer. With the remains of her half loaf tucked beneath her arm, she climbed to the laboratorium, uncertain whether he would welcome her or throw her down the stairs. She would tell him that she had not revealed his part in the plot, that his Great Work might proceed more slowly without the murderers' gold but it would proceed, and he would still have his head. And his immortal soul.

The laboratorium was cold and silent. Her father was not there. Neither were his books. Nor the glass instruments he called the pelican and the alembic. The fire was out. And the two sovereigns in the copper pot were gone.

Where was he? Had her plan failed? Had he been seized? Would she yet see his head on the bridge? Roger, she thought, that scurvy popinjay! This was all his fault. Had he helped her, they might have made a better plan.

Roger was useless. Whatever had he ever done for her? He had fed her, she admitted that. And he answered her questions . . . and admired her dark eyes . . . and found the baron's house. She remembered Roger's grin, his hair flopping in his eyes, his hand stretched out to help her over a puddle.

Ye toads and vipers, what had she done? This was not Roger's doing. He had ever been her friend, and she had been not generous, nor gentle, nor humble. She was filled with remorse.

Meggy was alone. Her father was gone, and she had driven Roger off. Her gran was dead, and her cold-hearted mother far away. Even Louise was taken from her. She flung herself down on her pallet and cried. In sooth she sobbed and wailed and bawled. She blubbered and sniveled. Finally, damp and exhausted, she wiped her nose, tied her linen cap on tighter, and hurried from the house. There was one thing she could remedy.

She pounded the bear's iron paw against the Grimms' front door, but no one answered. She asked at Ragwort's shop. The butcher shook his head in answer to her question and looked at her as if counting how many chops and ribs she might yield.

Meggy hurried away, up Pudding Lane, over to Gracechurch Street, and into the courtyard of the Cross Keys Inn. The yard was crowded not with scaffold and playgoers but with coaches and carts. "I wish to see the players," she said to a man holding a horse.

"There be no play today," said the man, and the horse neighed and nickered loudly. "Mayhap on the morrow, if they ain't been thrown into the Tower by then." He snickered, sounding much like his horse.

"I come not to see the play but the players," she said. "Do you know where they be?"

"Aye, I know," he said, then spat over his shoulder.

"Where then? Where are they?"

"They be . . . not here." He grinned. "That's where they be, Mistress Crookleg, they be . . . not here."

"Beef-witted churl," Meggy muttered as she hastened on. Where was Roger?

I know where he is, Meggy said to herself finally. 'Tis where I would go. And she hurried down to the river where they had eaten pigs' trotters and first talked of the baron. Certes he would be there, regretting their argument and ready to be friends again.

He was not there. A bitter wind blew refuse from the street into the air, dirt and pebbles peppered her skirt, and a sheet of paper plastered itself against her face.

It began to rain harder, and a sorrow-struck Meggy trudged slowly home. As she neared the house at the Sign of the Sun, she saw a man in a black gown enter. Her father safely come back! Relief flooded her, and she pushed open the door.

But it was not her father. Rather the man was a stranger. He turned toward Meggy. "Who are you and what do you in my house?" he asked her.

142

"What mean you, your house? This be the house of Master Ambrose, the alchemist, and I be his daught—"

"Nay, mistress, nay. Ambrose did sell this house and its contents to me last even'. He is off to Prague, in Bohemia, invited to join others in a place called Gold Alley, where alchemists gather. Did he not tell you?"

Meggy, speechless, shook her head.

"Oh, lucky Ambrose. Imagine. To work aside von Rosenberg, Hajek, the Baron Rodovsky." Disappointment shadowed the man's face. "If only it were possible, I would join them, but I have wife and children. Fortunate Ambrose, to be free and unencumbered."

Free? With a house and a daughter dwelling in it? He had left her without a farewell or a house or a father. Tears prickled at the back of Meggy's eyes, and her legs trembled.

"Here, mistress," said the stranger, pushing the stool toward her. "Sit a moment before you go . . . wherever you go. I must be about my business." He hummed tunelessly as he began measuring the walls and floors.

Meggy collapsed onto the stool. She thought her father had come to accept and even rely upon her. Of late she had tried to erase what he was and imagine him someone different, but in sooth he was heedless, cold, and uncaring.

You get no warmth from an empty fireplace, she thought, and she smiled to herself. She was becoming a philosopher. Empty fireplace indeed.

"I must be off, mistress," the stranger said. "I will be back anon with my family and expect to find you gone." He touched his cap in parting and added, "God save you and keep you well."

Once she was alone, Meggy, grief shot, put her head down on the table and wept again. She wept with despair and loneliness. She wept for what she almost had and had no longer, for what might have been. She was once again without a father. He had cared more for his alembic than his daughter, for he had taken that with him.

She wiped her face on her kirtle and straightened her cap. What was she to do? Go back to the mother who had sent her away? Find a likely spot in some stinking alley and beg?

Not I, said Meggy finally, banging a walking stick on the floor. I will tend to myself. She stood, pulled her cloak around her, and set off once more to see Master Allyn the printer.

Master Allyn was inking the leather balls when Meggy arrived. "See a new ballad come forth?" he called without turning around as she entered. "One moment and I will—

"Fie on it!" he shouted as the leather inking ball fell onto the dusty floor. He kicked the ball, and it flew to Meggy's feet.

"Master Allyn," said Meggy as she bent over and picked up the inking ball, "it appears you require my assistance." She handed the ball to him and wiped her inky hands on her kirtle. "I can help with Gilly and little Robert whilst Mistress Allyn tends the newest Allyn. I can ink the press, and you can teach me to pull letters for the composing stick. I can sell ballads throughout London, for my voice, though not sweet, is loud." Master Allyn started to interrupt her, but she silenced him with a wave. "I do not ask for wages. All I ask is a pallet by a fire and enough to eat, for I am ever cold and hungry." And lonely, she thought, although she did not say it.

"Nay, Mistress Meggy," said the printer when she paused. "Certes your father would not let you go."

"My father, such that he is, has abandoned me without a thought or a penny. I am free to go wherever . . . "

Master Allyn interrupted, frowning. "We will soon have three babes to care for. I dare not take on another."

"I do not require your care, Master Printer. I am offering my assistance in exchange for a pallet and supper."

"Pay heed to the girl, John," said Mistress Allyn from where she was hanging pages to dry, "for this new babe is soon coming, and I will be little use to you." She put a hand to the small of her back and stretched.

After a goodly silence, Master Allyn said to Meggy, "Be warned, I can be sharp and ill humored," but his eyes twinkled.

"No more than I, in truth," Meggy responded. "My friend Roger said I am as friendly as a bag of weasels. Mistress Crosspatch, he called me." Her eyes filled with tears again, and she dashed them away, leaving inky streaks on her cheeks.

"Then we are well matched," the printer said. "Welcome to the shop of John Allyn, Printer, off Paul's Chain, near Ludgate."

Meggy nodded. "Or," the printer added with a wink, "shall I say, 'John Allyn and Apprentice'?"

She nodded again as she wabbled to the shelves near the door, where she blew dust from a line of inking balls and straightened a stack of pages near to tumbling.

"I would say, John," Mistress Allyn said as she watched the girl, "it shall not be long before 'tis 'Mistress Swann and Printer.'"

Meggy smiled but she did not stop, for she had work to do.

✎ EIGHTEEN ✎

Meggy went one last time to the house at the Sign of the Sun to gather her things—comb, small knife for eating, clean smock, her scorched and tattered kirtle, a pair of stockings with the toes mended into a bunch, and a bottle of onion, fig, and Venice treacle tonic against plague, which mercifully she had not needed. She put them into her sack and took one last look around the cold, dark, empty room. How small it all was—small house, small room, small hopes, and even those had been disappointed. Farewell, Master Peevish, she thought, Sir Hardheart, Master Thoughtless. She wiped away fresh tears of loss and defeat as she walked once again to the printer's.

Meggy arrived to see a distinguished-looking man in fine gray doublet and blue trunk hose sitting by the fire. She could hear Mistress Allyn trying to quiet the children in the back room and saw the alarm on the printer's face. Her heart thumped.

"Here she is, the poet, as I told you," said Master Allyn to the gentleman.

The man looked doubtful. "This little girl with crooked legs—she is the maker of the ballad?"

Meggy's heart thumped again. It appeared her ballad was not the splendid idea she had thought it. "Aye, sir, I did write it," she said, almost in a whisper. "How came you here?"

"Your name was not on the broadside, but the printer's was." He looked from Meggy to Master Allyn. "You both be in grave trouble, meddling in treason."

Treason? Her heart pounded faster. "Nay, sir, I did but try to prevent treason. And Master Allyn had naught to do with it. 'Twas all my doing." Was she about to be taken to prison? To Newgate or the Clink? Or even the Tower? She lifted one hand to touch her hair, as if assuring herself that her head was still on her shoulders and not on a pole on London Bridge.

"The queen takes threats to her nobles as threats to the Crown itself. Tell me," the gentleman said, narrowing his eyes, "what have you to do with this plot against the baron?"

"Naught, sir, naught."

"The truth!" the man shouted, pounding his hand on the arm of the chair. "Tell me the truth!"

"Hold, good sir, hold!" Master Allyn said, coming to Meggy's side. "The girl—"

"Be still!" the gentleman said. "Let her answer me."

Meggy trembled, but her voice was strong. "I am telling the truth, sir. I had naught to do with the plot. I did but overhear the redheaded man and his gorbellied friend speak of their plans, and there was no other way to warn the baron. The gatekeeper would not let me pass, and I could not fly over the baron's walls and sing a song at his window." Meggy sighed, remembering Roger's foolery that had belike given her the idea for the ballad.

"Know you the baron?"

"Oh, no, sir. How could I know a baron?"

"Why then were you part of this? Who put you up to it?" He stood and wagged his finger in Meggy's face. "Were you paid? By whom?"

Meggy backed away. "Oh, no, sir. Naught and no one and ne'er!" she said, speaking as quickly as she could as if to forestall any more questions. "I but knew it was wrong, sir, to plot murder. And that I should stop it if I could. And the red-headed man was so ugly and venomous, with a foul reek like a toad in a dung pile, that I knew the matter must be most wicked indeed were he at the heart of it."

The gentleman looked as though he would like to smile but had forgotten how. He sat back down and spoke more gently. "The threat to the baron was real," he said. "His food taster and your redheaded toad have been removed to the Tower, although certes there were other plotters." Meggy let out a breath she did not know she had been holding. Fortunate it was that her father had gone to Bohemia. He was safe. Gone, but safe.

"What more do you know?" The gentleman had still more questions. "Have you heard aught else?"

"Naught, sir. I swear. That is the whole and entire tale." She hoped God would forgive her lie, but she would not reveal her father's role. She would not.

The man got to his feet. "In sooth, I do not find that you two were involved with the plot. Indeed, young bard, you may have saved the baron's life. Belike he will want to offer some small reward. What would you have from the baron in thanks?"

A reward? Meggy's head spun as she tried to think. Gold? Fine clothes? A silver bracelet? Grass green shoes? In truth there was little she truly needed, she realized. She had a pallet by the fire and the promise of enough to eat. Her father was safely gone. She would like Roger back but did not think that was a matter for the baron. But there was something. She mourned the lost possibility of such fine shoes and explained her wish to the gentleman.

"I can but ask," the gentleman said. And, with a bow, he left.

For two wet and windy days, Meggy trudged from one end of London to another, singing ballads and hawking broadsides. Some folks were unkind to her, as ever, but others were friendly. Although her legs still ached, she was stronger and wearied less easily. But so much traveling left her hands blistered and raw. Mayhap, she thought, the cooper could smooth her sticks so they would not tear at her hands so. She once again made the walk to Crooked Lane.

As she turned down the lane from Candlewick Street, she could smell the spice-cake smell that meant the cooper was firing oak casks. Her mouth watered at the aroma. As important as casks and barrels were, she could not help but wish it truly were spice cake he was baking.

A wagon was drawn up in front of the house at the Sign of the Sun, and a carter was moving barrels and boxes in. Laughter streamed out the open door. Meggy thought of her own very different arrival some months ago. She stood staring at the house for a moment, remembering what was and imagining what might have been, and then she turned to the cooper's.

The cooper's shop was free of charred wood and ashes although the beams and the walls were still blackened from the fire. In one corner the cooper was busily smoothing barrel staves, and Nicholas played with his horse in a mound of sawdust. Meggy explained to the cooper why she had come. "Ah, Mistress Meggy, I can do better than that," he said. From the back of his shop he brought out a pair of walking sticks, fine oak and polished until they were like satin. The tops of the T shapes were padded with leather. "To thank you, mistress, for your kindness to my boy."

Meggy grinned as she tried them out. With these fine new sticks, she was steadier and stood taller, and—wonder of wonders—her hands did not hurt.

"How fares your beauteous goose?" Nicholas asked Meggy as she paced the length of the shop. "Where is she? Do you miss her? Shall she be coming back to Crooked Lane?"

"Soft, Master Nicholas, soft. Louise does dwell now with someone else, and aye, I miss her and her squawks and her waddles."

"I do wish I waddled like you and Louise," the boy said, watching Meggy. "It be most like dancing."

Meggy was astounded at his words. She had ever thought her lameness ugly and her wabbles ungraceful, but her gait in truth was a bit of swaying and a bit of bobbling and joggling. In some measure like dancing indeed.

"Someone came seeking you this very morning," Master Cooper said. Meggy's heart leapt. Roger! "A tall, scar-faced man." Not Roger. Master Merryman.

Meggy thanked the cooper and headed for Pudding Lane to see what Master Merryman wanted of her. In truth she hoped to find Roger there. Roger. Her heart lurched back and forth between joy and dismay at the thought of seeing again that big nose and foolish grin.

❦ N I N E T E E N ❧

One of Master Grimm's apprentices opened the door. Inside was a crowd of people—apprentices, Master and Mistress Grimm, Master Merryman, all the Grimm children, Francis Shore the fencing master, and a number of men she remembered seeing in the play but had not yet met—laughing and talking.

"Mistress Swann," Mistress Grimm, coming to Meggy's side, said over the bibble-babble. "Sweeting, we have been looking for you but no one knew where you had gone."

"Wherefore this celebration?" Meggy asked her.

Master Grimm's voice rang over the others. "I have no doubt it was my performance in *Master Gamecock and the Death of the King* that convinced the baron to give us this opportunity. In sooth, who could have watched my Master Gamecock and not been moved?"

"Our fortunes have taken a goodly turn," Mistress Grimm said. "I will let Merryman tell you, for he was there." They pushed through the crowded and noisy room to where

Master Merryman leaned against the fireplace, smiling his sad smile.

"Mistress Swann," he said, "well met. You are just in time for our festive gathering."

"What and why do you celebrate?" Meggy asked. "No one yet has said."

"It appears that Sir Mortimer Blunt, the baron Eastmoreland, has commanded a performance of us. He had his fellows call on us this very day. If we please him, belike he will give us his patronage and a license to play." He smiled his sad smile at the girl.

"Mistress, have you heard?" Master Grimm shouted over the noise. "We are to be Sir Mortimer's Men, for I am sure we will please him. Our future will be assured and our fortune made!"

So the baron had done as she had asked! "'Tis good news indeed, Master Grimm, Master Merryman, and well deserved." Meggy remembered how swept up she had been in the play she had seen. If the baron was moved as much, the company would be Sir Mortimer's Men without fail.

She felt warm with the knowledge that she had been of such assistance to people who had been kind to her. But she had something more on her mind. "Where is Roger?" she asked. "I do not see him."

Mistress Grimm gestured to the door. "The pigeon-livered boy went into the kitchen when he saw you come. He says you two are angry."

Meggy hurried to the kitchen. There was Roger sitting at the table, piercing an apple over and over with his knife.

"Leave off torturing that apple, Oldmeat," Meggy said. "It has done you no wrong. It was I."

He looked up. "Go away," he said.

"I have come to say I am sorry. Pray pardon me for—"

"Get you gone."

"But, Roger, I beg you to—"

"Leave me!"

"Will you not even listen and give me—"

Roger stuck the knife deep into the heart of the apple. "Go away, Meggy Swann. I wish to hold on to my anger yet for a time before I forgive you."

Relief flooded Meggy like warm soup. He would forgive her. They would be friends again. "You were right, Roger, to say what you did. I am indeed a selfish, ungrateful girl, and I cry your mercy. I will try to improve. After all, you are my only friend who is not a goose."

"Only friend?" Roger gestured toward the other room. "Are you not now among friends? You no longer be the solitary, sorrowful girl who first came, although your bad temper remains, as I can attest."

Meggy considered his words. Was she so changed? Just when had that happened, and how?

Roger led her back to the parlor. "Mistress Grimm," cried Master Grimm, "this good fortune has made me hungry. My empty belly rumbles like a cart. Bring us beer and bread, apples and nuts." He put his arm around Master Merryman's shoulder. "My good friend and fellow player Dick Merryman will stand treat, will you not, Dick?"

Master Merryman winked at Mistress Grimm. "Indeed, Cuthbert, indeed," he replied, and she turned for the kitchen.

The company resumed their rejoicing. The little Grimm girls danced about the room like spinning toys. The apprentices slapped one another's backs and punched one another's shoulders. One of them began to sing a wordless song with a tootling tune.

And Meggy, caught up in the joyous spirit, began to sing a celebration song she had learned of her gran:

> *Good fellows must go learn to dance*
> *Thy bride-ale's full near-a.*
> *There is a dance come out of France*
> *The first ye heard this year-a.*

Master Grimm swung Ivory Silk (or was it Silver Damask?) around, Master Merryman led Violet Velvet in a stately dance, and Roger leapt and twirled with Russet Wool in his arms. The apprentices laughed and whooped, "By my faith, a fine song!" and "More, Mistress Meggy, more!" so Meggy gave them more:

> *For I must leap and thou must hop*
> *And we must turn all three-a*

The fourth must bounce like a top,
And so we shall agree-a.
I pray thee, minstrel, make no stop
For we will merry be-a.

Roger put the baby down and clapped excitedly. "Who else has a song? Who else?" he called.

"You sing for us, my dear," said Master Grimm to his wife, who was returning with great mugs of ale. "Let us have 'The Fair Maid of Islington,' as you sang it when first I wooed you."

Mistress Grimm protested but finally said, "For you, Cuthbert, on this happy day." She began to sing:

There was a youth, a well-beloved youth,
And he was a squire's son.
He loved the bailiff's daughter dear
That lived in Islington.

In truth she twittered and twangled and wheezed, but it was enough like singing that the others clapped and danced.

Meggy was happy for them, but she felt suddenly alone, knowing that her own father had discarded her like an outworn shoe.

Russet Wool, crawling on the floor, had found Meggy's sack and busily pulled out the broadsides. At the bottom he found Meggy's scorched and ragged kirtle, wadded into a ball, and he shook it about until it opened out and, with a thud, hit his head. He began to cry.

Thud? Meggy wondered as Mistress Grimm picked Russet up and comforted him. How is it my kirtle thuds?

Meggy sat down on a bench, the kirtle in her lap. Something was knotted in the hem. When she untied the knot, a small parcel fell onto the floor, a parcel wrapped in a page torn from a book, and on that page was written *Margret*.

She tore off the paper to find a large gold coin. A sovereign. One of the two sovereigns her father had been paid by the assassins. The Tudor rose on its surface winked at her, and her belly filled with both joy and sadness.

Her father had not left her without a thought. Selfish he might be, and remote, and consumed by his work, even a fraud and a murderer, but he was not indifferent to her. He had not much to give, but he had shared it with her. Her eyes filled with tears again, and she clutched the coin tightly. "Naught matters but my work," he had said. "Naught." But he had left a coin for her. And he had, after all, known her name.

Farewell, sir, she thought. And then, Farewell, Father. And Godspeed.

She slipped the coin into her sack. She would not spend it, she decided, not be enriched from gains so ill-gotten, but would keep it as a remembrance. It was all she had of him. No, not quite all. A coin and her black eyes and, she admitted, her curiosity, stubbornness, and persistence.

While Violet Velvet sang "Bonny Sweet Robin," Mistress Grimm danced with Russet Wool, the bump on his head forgotten. Meggy looked on in envy. Had she ever had such warmth and care from her own mother? No, all warmth, all kindness, all gentleness had come from her gran. She had naught from her cold, ungenerous mother. Well, mayhap her sharp tongue . . . her suspicious nature . . . a skill at bargaining, and—she smiled—a great many words of insult. Even Louise had given the girl something, the knowledge that one did not have to be perfect to be beauteous. All these—and, in sooth, her own cleverness and fierce determination—had led to this day, she realized. She had friends, a place of her own choosing, the promise of plenty to eat. She was rich indeed.

"Meggy, Meggy, come dance with us," the twins shouted, pulling at her. While Violet Velvet sang on, Meggy spread her arms wide and leaned on her new sticks, and the girls threaded themselves under and around and under again, laughing and singing along, *My Robin loves me, aye, he does.* She lifted one leg and twirled round on the other, and back again. She swayed and bobbled and joggled.

There she was, Meggy Swann, dancing! Her linen cap flew off, and her hair spun and tangled and found its way into her eyes and her mouth. She looked around as she twirled, part of a scene of joy and friendship and gaiety. Ye toads and vipers, here was transformation indeed! Master Merryman nodded his approval of her dance, and Roger winked. Meggy laughed. She, Meggy Swann, the formerly ugglesome crookleg, the foul-featured cripple, she was dancing!

❦ AUTHOR'S NOTE ❧

Queen Elizabeth I of England has lent her name to an extraordinary period in Western history. The Elizabethan era, from her accession to the throne in 1558 until her death in 1603, was a proud time for England. The land was united and mostly at peace. It was the age of the Renaissance, of new ideas and new thinking, artistic brilliance and daring exploration. European wars brought continental refugees into England, exposing the English to new cultures and under-standings. Advances in printing made books more available to both scholars and ordinary people. Poets, playwrights, and musicians produced works of enduring beauty and power.

Laboratory experiments resulted in advances in natural philosophy, which would later be called science, although such pursuits as astrology and alchemy were still taken seriously by educated people. Alchemy was not an Elizabethan, or even European, invention; people over the globe and over the centuries searched for the secrets of the universe. Alchemy had roots in Mesopotamia, Egypt, Persia, India, Japan, Korea, and China, in classical Greece and Rome, and in the empires of Islam. Much of the existing material about alchemy reflects a mixture of scientific experimentation with the supernatural. These writings are often deliberately obscure, as alchemists balanced the need to communicate with their desire to pro-tect alchemical secrets.

Alchemy is based on the idea that the world is composed of four elements: fire, earth, water, and air. The eighth-century Islamic alchemist Geber analyzed each element in terms of four basic qualities: hotness, coldness, dryness, and moistness. Fire was hot and dry, earth cold and dry, water cold and moist, and air hot and moist. Geber theorized that every metal was a combination of these four principles and so reasoned that the transmutation of one metal into another could be effected by the rearrangement of its basic qualities. To do this, one would need the help of the philosopher's stone.

The illusory philosopher's stone was thought to be a magical substance capable of turning lumps of inexpensive metals into gold. It was also believed to be an elixir of life, or panacea, useful for healing, for rejuvenation, and possibly for achieving immortality. It is said that many alchemists tested their discoveries on themselves and died of mercury, silver, or lead poisoning. Master Ambrose's beliefs and the experiments that he carries out in his laboratorium are all based on what I could understand from ancient and modern writings about alchemy.

Alchemists, of course, never turned base metal to gold. They did, however, invent procedures, processes, and equipment that showed later generations how to analyze minerals and metals and make medicines from them, how to distill essences, how chemical changes follow from combining different substances, how to use balances and weights, and how to build and use a variety of laboratory vessels. Alchemy's significant advances laid the basis for the science of chemistry.

◇ ◇ ◇

In the centuries before there were newspapers and news channels, the general public had to rely on news from the street to find out what was happening. The most popular news medium in England from the sixteenth to the mid-nineteenth century was the broadside. Sold by street vendors and sometimes pinned up on walls in shops and alehouses, these single sheets carried public notices, news, speeches, and songs that could be read or sung aloud. The first broadsides were printed to inform the public of royal proclamations, acts, and official notices. Later they covered themes ranging from politics to current events.

Broadsides were mainly pages of text, but occasionally illustrations were added. Generally the illustrations were crude woodcuts and, in many cases, bore little or no relation to the text.

Some broadsides offered accounts of murders and descriptions of executions, including a supposed confession by the guilty party and his or her last words. Many, if not all, of these scaffold speeches and confessions were purely fictional descriptions of how the condemned fell into a life of crime. They'd end with a plea for forgiveness and an appeal to the reader to live an upright life.

Broadsides about storms, shipwrecks, floods, and fires were as popular as newspaper stories about such disasters are today. So too were accounts of "monstrous" children and sightings of mermaids, cannibals, and sea monsters, which included dates, names, and places to give the impression that these were true events.

The most common form of the broadside was the ballad. Ballads were poems or songs, meant to be sung, about romance, historical persons and events, the private lives of politicians and royalty, new legislation, unpopular taxes, the supernatural, and even sports. Among the earliest ballad broadsides was "A Lytel Geste of Robyne Hood," printed in 1506. Famous writers such as Robert Burns produced ballads, but generally the words appeared anonymously. The tunes were usually old favorites with new words. New tunes were merely suggested on the sheets, for only a small number of broadsides printed had musical notation. Street balladry was a popular form of entertainment, as well as a method for providing the latest news. Most of the ballads were sung by hawkers who sold the printed version for a halfpenny or a penny.

Many of the printers who produced broadsides would also have printed chapbooks, hornbooks, sermons, and playbills. Sometimes the printers distributed their own wares, but they usually relied on ballad sellers—peddlers who would sing and shout on the streets about the latest publication or carry newly printed materials to markets and fairs throughout England.

The ballads and broadsides in *Alchemy and Meggy Swann*, with the exception of Meggy's own ballad and Roger's silly song, are quoted from or based upon actual broadsides from the sixteenth and seventeenth centuries. Many of these can be seen as facsimiles on various sites on the Internet, a situation that would surely astonish the ballad singers and sellers of the past.

Meggy Swann lives at a time when many medieval ideas and prejudices are disappearing, including certain attitudes toward the ill, infirm, or disabled. Although opinions were diverse, most people believed that such afflictions had supernatural or demonological causes. Ill or disabled persons might be suffering possession or intervention by the Devil or perhaps God's punishment for some unspecified sin. But the times were changing. The Fourth Lateran Council of the Church in 1215 had found that illness or impairment was only *sometimes* caused by sin. The birth of the modern era and the development of scientific and medical theories saw more advocates for belief in natural causes.

Seriously ill or disabled people were mainly taken care of in hospitals and infirmaries operated by the Catholic Church. But after Henry VIII dissolved the monasteries and dispersed the priests in the mid-sixteenth century, the ill and infirm often found themselves on the streets, forced to beg. In 1601 England passed a so-called Poor Law to codify care for the needy. Those unable to work—the lame, elderly, and blind and very young children—were to be cared for in almshouses, or poorhouses. The able-bodied poor were to be set to work in a workhouse, called a house of industry. Vagrants or the idle poor could be sent to a house of corrections or even prison. Even so, beggars swarmed the streets.

Before I could tell Meggy's story, I needed to know exactly what her disability was, how it affected her, and how it looked to other people. I decided she suffered from what is now called bilateral hip dysplasia, an abnormal formation of both hip joints at birth in which the ball at the top of each thighbone is not stable in the socket. Unless this is corrected soon after birth, abnormal stresses cause malformation of the developing bone, and the child will have difficulty walking, a characteristic limp or waddling gait, and, if untreated, life-long pain. The condition can be inherited or caused by the baby being carried in an unsuitable position in the womb or being born in the breech position (especially with feet up by the shoulders).

In Meggy's time, little was known about how to identify hip dysplasia and even less how to treat it. Children now are routinely examined for it at birth. The condition can be treated with physical therapy and medications, braces and splints, or surgery.

Louise's slipped wing, also known as angel wing, crooked wing, or drooped wing, is a condition of ducks and geese where the last joint of the wing is twisted so that the wing feathers point outward rather than lying smooth against the body. The birds that develop the problem are perfectly healthy, but, according to one Internet site, "they are just not as beautiful." I'm certain that Nicholas would disagree.

In Elizabethan as in medieval England, the words *thee* and *thou* were used as well as *you. Thee* and *thou* were familiar or informal forms of *you*. One used them to address children, servants, family, and closest friends. Many people today think that *thou* is the more formal word because it is used in the King James Version of the Bible when someone is speaking to God. However, the translators of the King James Version wanted the reader to know that one's relationship to God is personal and familiar, and so they used *thou*.

The more formal *you* was used to address strangers and anyone above one in rank. It was also used as a sign of respect to one's parents or elders. The plural of *you* was *ye*—completely different from the *ye* meaning *the*, which is pronounced *the*.

By the end of the sixteenth century, those grammatical rules were breaking down. Most people, including Shakespeare, used *you* and *thou* interchangeably. I decided that the language in *Alchemy and Meggy Swann* was complicated enough without the additional pronouns, so I have used only *you*, as we do now.

If you want to know more about the historical setting of Meggy's story, here are some places to look:

Davis, William Stearns. *Life in Elizabethan Days: A Picture of a Typical English Community at the End of the Sixteenth Century.* New York: Harper & Bros., 1930.

Emerson, Kathy Lynn. *The Writer's Guide to Everyday Life in Renaissance England.* Cincinnati: Writer's Digest Books, 1996.

Moran, Bruce T. *Distilling Knowledge: Alchemy, Chemistry, and the Scientific Revolution.* Cambridge, Mass.: Harvard University Press, 2005.

Picard, Liza. *Elizabeth's London: Everyday Life in Elizabethan London.* New York: St. Martin's Press, 2004.

Stow, John. *A Survey of London Written in the Year 1598.* Dover, N.H.: Alan Sutton Publishers, 1994.

Woog, Adam. *A History of the Elizabethan Theater.* San Diego: Lucent Books, 2003.

www.elizabethan.org

www.elizabethi.org

mapoflondon.uvic.ca

Read all of Karen Cushman's books!

THE MIDWIFE'S APPRENTICE

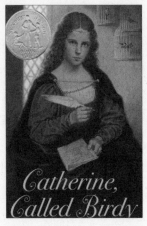

CATHERINE, CALLED BIRDY

MATILDA BONE

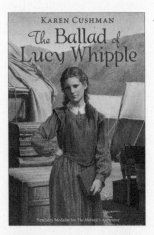

THE BALLAD OF LUCY WHIPPLE